The Carpathian Shadows: Volume II

Edited by Lea Schizas

Stories by: Carol A. Cole, Kristin Johnson, Kevin R. Tipple, Christina Barber, Seana Graham, Donna Amato

BooksForABuck.com

2008

The Carpathian Shadows: Volume Two

Edited by Lea Schizas
Stories by: Carol A. Cole, Kristin Johnson,
Kevin R. Tipple, Christina Barber,
Seana Graham, Donna Amato

Published by BooksForABuck.com

October, 2008

ISBN: 978-1-60215-087-4

CONTENTS

Forward by Lea Schizas

Publisher's Note

A Visitor From the Past by Carol A. Cole

Divine Curse by Kristin Johnson

By the Light Of the Moon… by Kevin R. Tipple

Thicker Than Stone by Christina Barber

The Scholar by Seana Graham

Hear No Evil, Speak No Evil by Donna Amato

Acknowledgements

Carol A. Cole: All my thanks to Kathie Coyne who first encouraged me to write, Karen Miller, my first editor, Karen Omartian and Chris Fleming, both long-time friends who dutifully read my early stories and of course to my wonderful husband, Bob and son, Robert who put up with me tapping away at the computer at all hours.

Kristin Johnson: To the incredible Lea, whose edits were incisive and invaluable. To the wonderful Carpathian Shadows authors. To the MuseItUpClub, which brings us back to Lea and brings together some of the best talent I've ever encountered. And most of all to my family.

Kevin R. Tipple: Dedicated to my parents, Karl and Elvia Netta Tipple, my brother, Karl Regan Tipple, my wife Sandi, and my own sons, Karl and Scott. Thank you for your love and support in all things.

Seana Graham: Many thanks to Lea Schizas for her tireless efforts on behalf of the writing community and on this project in particular. And to Bram Stoker, who put Transylvania on the map of our collective imagination.

Donna Amato: Thanks to Lea Schizas for this incredible opportunity and her untiring efforts to help new writers. And to my children, Jaime, Danielle, Jeremy and Josh whose confidence in me has helped me achieve my success as a writer. Thank you.

Foreword

Vampires, werewolves, zombies… all legendary creatures hunting their preys, all containing their own personal tales and backgrounds.

But the most evasive story to be told is that of Lord John Erdely from the Carpathian Mountains in Transylvania, Romania.

Lord John Erdely lived in the 17th century and date of death cannot be confirmed since no body has ever been found. It is rumored, but no documents support this theory, that he dealt in black magic to suppress the ongoing collaboration of the churches to bring a unified religion to all people, a Greek Catholic practice.

It is also rumored he may have used black magic to contain his servants, to blind and deafen them from words spoken to them while on errands for the Lord within the village of Cornifu. Villagers became increasingly suspicious of Lord Erdely when family members went missing.

Enter the present time…

All visitors staying in Cornifu Hotel are surprised with a mystery invitation for a one-day excursion to Erdely Castle. Befuddled but amused at the same time, they accept, unaware of the events to follow.

Join our characters as each discovers secrets and mysteries that will change their lives forever.

Lea Schizas
Carol A. Cole
Kristin Johnson
Kevin R. Tipple
Christina Barber
Seana Graham
Donna Amato

Publisher's Note

I hope you enjoy Volume Two of THE CARPATHIAN SHADOWS as much as I did. The stories trick you into thinking you understand what's going on—let you think that the characters are entering a different world once they reach Lord Erdely's castle. Alert readers will be rewarded, though. Is the small hotel in Cornifu really as simple as it seems to be? Why does the tourist bus seem to have a different group of tourists with every trip—or is it really only one trip? And who is the mysterious and ever-bubbly 'American' tour leader, Jennifer Brooks? Lord Erdely, too, seems to take different forms, as if the present can alter the past itself.

Only one thing is certain as we enter the shadows of the Carpathian Mountains—and the bloody history that they represent: nobody getting on that friendly tour bus will emerge unchanged.

A Visitor From the Past
By
Carol A. Cole

"Mr. Collier, there's mail for you." The hotel Cornifu desk clerk waved an envelope at Rob as he and Anna entered the small hotel lobby.

"Who knows we're here?" Anna pulled a scarf off her hair.

"Maybe someone from the office. You know how Adam is. Only working vacations for Williams and Company employees." Rob took the letter and they headed for the staircase.

"But it's our anniversary. Even vice-presidents deserve some down-time." Anna snatched the letter and stormed up the steps to their room.

Rob stared after his wife of twenty-five years, his college sweetheart. This was their long-awaited vacation to all the out-of-the-way cities in Europe. He and Anna had talked about and planned the trip for five years, but she seemed different lately. She wasn't excited about the older hotels they'd booked or talked about the next city on their list.

Anna had been quick-tempered with him and their two dogs ever since she returned from a business trip to Germany fourteen months ago. She'd even had her waist-length hair that he loved since the day he met her, cut off on the trip. Always before, she would brush it out at night, sitting on the edge of their four-poster bed. He loved to see it splayed across the crisp white pillowcase while she slept. "Why did you get it cut so short?" he'd asked.

"It's too much to bother with," she'd snapped. Later, she apologized. "This last trip was just too tiring, although I did visit a wonderful Cathedral in Bonn. I wish you could have seen the stained glass windows. It was breathtaking. It took several decades to complete."

Rob hoped this trip would rekindle their relationship.

****

Rob entered their room and spied the letter tossed on the bed.

Anna stood at the window gazing at the mountains in the distance.

"You okay, hon?" He gently rubbed her shoulders and upper back.

Anna stiffened slightly then leaned into his body. "I'm just tired. Maybe we can turn in early after dinner tonight. I'm looking forward visiting the cathedral in Brasov tomorrow. Did you know work stopped on it several times and it wasn't finished until 1654?"

Rob kissed her gently behind her left ear, a particularly sensitive spot, but Anna didn't respond. He sat on the bed, tore open the envelope, and read the letter aloud.

Dear Robert and Anna Collier:

We cordially invite you for a free tour within the famous castle of Lord Erdely.

Our guide, Jennifer Brooks, will be departing tomorrow at 8am sharp from Hotel Cornifu for this one-day excursion we have planned.

Visit the mysterious surroundings of the Erdely Castle and see for yourself if it is indeed haunted.

Yours truly,
Bruce Campbell
President of The American Paranormal Association of World Tours

"There was something in the tour book about Erdely Castle. I believe it was also built around the 1650's."

"How did they get our names?" Anna asked, glaring at the letter. Rob had always shown an interest in ghosts and haunted buildings. "How did they know we were here? Did you sign up for this before we left?"

"No, I've never heard of them, but I have read about the castle. I understood it was closed to visitors. This is a great opportunity."

"Not another ghost hunt," Anna muttered. She'd gone with him to a supposedly haunted house back home and wasn't convinced there were ghosts there. "You promised we could visit the cathedral." She stood in front of him playing with the hair curling on top of his shirt collar. Gently stroking his cheek, Anna slid the letter out of his hand then pushed him down onto the bed. "I'm not really hungry. Maybe we could skip dinner all together," she whispered in his ear.

Reaching up, Rob pulled Anna next to him. "You were starving when we finished the museum tour." His stomach suddenly rumbled and he laughed. "Now, I'm starving. We can eat in the dining room downstairs and finish this for dessert." He sat up and reached for the letter, which had fallen to the floor. "The letter says the tour is free. We can visit the cathedral on Friday. I'm sure we can extend our reservation here another night. I think half the rooms are vacant."

"There are some nice shops here in town, maybe you could go on the tour, and I could sleep in and then do some shopping." Anna looked toward the window. "I am tired and wouldn't be much company on a ghost hunt."

"Just because you don't believe in the spirits doesn't make the trip worthless. The castle's bound to be interesting architecturally." He ruffled her hair and wrapped his arms around her.

"I…I really don't want to see it," Anna whispered as something cold touched the back of her neck.

"Please." Rob hugged her tightly to him. "I really want you to come with me. It's our anniversary trip."

Anna leaned into his embrace and sighed. "All right, one ghost tour on the schedule."

"Great." He gave her a quick kiss before standing up. Folding the letter, he placed it in his jacket pocket and grabbed the room key. "Let's see what the menu has to offer." He held out his hand and Anna rose slowly and walked with him to the door.

* * * *

After a quick breakfast, Rob and Anna joined a small group in front of the Hotel. Several other couples and a few single tourists, most of them American, each held identical letters from Bruce Campbell.

Rob chatted about Lord Erdely with one of the men while Anna stood off by herself until a tour bus pulled up to the front of the hotel.

A smiling woman with brunette hair swinging across her shoulders bounced down the bus steps. "Good morning, everyone. I'm Jennifer Brooks and I'll be your guide on today's tour. Our driver is Vlad Mysecki. If you could give me your names as you board the bus, we'll be on our way."

When the first couple greeted the driver, Jennifer spoke up. "Vlad is deaf, I'm afraid and can only lip read words in Romanian. Don't worry; he's a very capable driver." She quickly checked off everyone's name and the bus pulled away from the hotel.

Jennifer stepped to the front of the bus and turned on her microphone. "Ladies and gentlemen, I'd like to welcome you to Transylvania—which translates to 'the land beyond the forest'. Before we head to the castle, our tour will take us into the surrounding countryside. We will be passing several walled cities or citadels built by German settlers who emigrated from Saxony in the twelfth century. I apologize for the bumpy ride through the town, but the Romanian people have kept the cobblestone streets as well as the defense towers as a reminder of their history."

She smiled at the passengers. "The Eastern Europeans are not as quick to embrace the modern world as we are in America. You will find many of the colorful houses date back several centuries."

The bus sped along the road and Rob gazed at the fields of wildflowers beginning to fade in the crisp autumn air, and the snow capped Fagaras Mountains in the distance. He clasped Anna's hand and kissed her cheek. "Thank you for coming on my ghost hunt."

She smiled at him, returned the kiss, and turned back to the window.

"Mr. Collier, what brings you and your wife to Transylvania?" Jennifer had been walking down the aisle asking each tour guest.

"My wife and I are celebrating our twenty-fifth anniversary. We toured the major cities of Europe on our honeymoon and wanted to see the sites hidden away in the back of the tour books. Anna is an architect and loves searching out old cathedrals such as the Saint Nicolae in Brasov and the Catholic Cathedral in Oradea. We rent a car and just drive until we discover something to explore."

Jennifer glanced at Mrs. Collier who had avoided joining in their conversation. "I hope you both enjoy today's tour of the castle; it has some beautiful architectural features unique to the time period." She moved to another couple while Anna stared out the window at the oak and beech woods that lined the narrowing road.

"If you look out the left side of the bus, you will see Moldoveanu, Romania's highest peak at 8,343 feet. There are also several wineries to our north in Jidvei."

Several minutes later, the bus passed the road that led back to Cornifu and turned up a steep hill. "We should be arriving at Lord Erdely's Castle momentarily." Jennifer announced. "His servants used to walk down from the castle to do their marketing."

* * * *

Stepping off the bus, Rob stretched his legs and looked back down the narrow dirt road that led from the highway to the castle grounds. "I'd hate to have to walk down that road in the dark; the bus ride was bad enough," he whispered to Anna.

Anna stared at the imposing stone structure almost hidden by the wild growth of vines and fir trees and slowly walked forward as if drawn toward the castle.

"The outer walls of the castle are fourteen feet thick and forty feet high," Jennifer's voice could be heard near the bus.

Rob followed Anna to the castle. The aged stone walls soared overhead and tilting his head back he could just make out the spires blending in with the branches of the trees. The azure blue sky darkened and he felt the temperature drop. Reaching for Anna's hand he whispered, "Let's join the others." The group had reached the front of the castle and Jennifer pulled open one of the heavy, carved wooden doors.

Glancing back toward the bus, Rob saw Vlad close the doors and turn the bus toward the dirt road. "Is he leaving?"

Jennifer nodded her head and laughed. "Vlad's seen the castle many times. He usually drives back down the hill and has lunch while we're on the tour. Don't worry; he'll be back in time to pick us up this afternoon." She turned to the rest of the tour group and motioned for them to enter the castle. "We'll tour the first two floors before lunch in the great hall, and visit the towers and grounds after eating."

The group entered the castle and gathered by the bottom of a vast stone staircase circling toward the upper levels. Two old knight's suits of armor flanked the first step with another on the landing.

Rob stared at the huge tapestries hanging on the walls. They depicted life in the fifteen hundreds and resembled the paintings in fine museums. One scene pictured three oxen roasting on spits in a huge stone oven with several pigs and chickens in a pen outside the medieval kitchen. Another showed the tower dungeon with a young man chained to a pillar.

Anna gently touched the stone walls and even giggled when Rob had to duck going up the narrow curved staircase to the next level. There, one of the restored bedchambers held a large wooden-framed bed with a white linen canopy overhead and a thick feather mattress. Rough-spun cloth and a fine woolen blanket lay across the foot of the bed. Several huge logs filled the fireplace and a chamber pot sat on a wooden stool next to the bed. Several candles burned in sconces hanging on the walls.

"Guests of Lord John Erdely would have slept in bedrooms such as this with the lords and ladies in separate accommodations. Their servants would have slept on benches or palettes on the floor in the same rooms to be near if needed." Jennifer pointed out the small openings in the inner wall of the room. "These peepholes or squints were used to see the activities in the floors below.

As they moved back downstairs, Jennifer continued with the known history of Lord Erdely. "The Lord was an avowed atheist who had many clashes with the Greek Church at that time. The villagers in Cornifu spread rumors that Erdely used black magic to keep his servants from hearing the talk in town about the collaboration of the churches to bring a unified religion to the people. Often many months went by between visits between Erdely's servants and their family members in the town."

Entering the great hall, Anna pointed out the silk wall hangings and the larger windows lining one wall. She grabbed Rob's hand and led him to sit on one of the small stone benches. "The castles were usually very dark, so these windows were larger to let in the light and also afford the residents and guests a view of the countryside."

Rob hugged Anna to him, glad she appeared to be enjoying the tour. "You could probably tell Jennifer more about the architecture of the buildings than she already knows."

"It's not really any different than other castles from this time period." She shrugged and stood. "The linen on the tables would have been brought back from visiting other cities; these tables resemble the rough-hewn wood of that time."

"What about the chandeliers?" Rob glanced at the heavy iron fixture suspended from the ceiling. Two rows of bulbs shaped like candle flames circled the edge.

"Of course they would have been real candles back then, but the fixture itself could date back to Lord Erdely's time."

"Lunch is ready," Jennifer stated, entering the hall.

Rob and Anna joined the others at the long table where they found place cards inscribed with their names. Large loaves of dark bread sat on wooden planks while covered tureens alternated with platters of roast turkey drumsticks. Jugs of wine and water were placed near the dishes.

"This isn't quite a medieval banquet, but the Association tries to be inconspicuous as possible, so they set up the lunch while we were upstairs and have left for the day."

* * * *

After they finished the meal and stacked their dishes on a rolling cart, which Jennifer pushed into the kitchen, the group moved to the rear of the castle. A replica of an ancient herb garden sat next to a fenced-in area.

Anna shivered and hung back from the group.

"Are you okay?" Rob asked.

"Just cold; it looks like rain." Anna's face had paled and she glanced nervously as the group headed up a small hill. "I think I want to go back and sit down. Come with me."

"I'll just take a quick peek at the garden and be right back." Rob moved to the rear of the group.

"Lord Erdely's servants would slaughter the animals kept in this pen and use the herbs from the garden to flavor the meals. The kitchen help would often go into town to buy the wine and sweets served to guests." Jennifer led the group through the garden. "The trees behind the castle would be cut down and used for furniture as well as firewood."

A loud clap of thunder startled the group and the sky opened up pouring down cold rain. "Let's get back inside." Jennifer directed them toward the door. "This is unusual for this time of year. It should be a short rain. We'll visit the towers and continue the outside tour when it stops."

* * * *

The deluge continued all afternoon. After touring two of the towers, Jennifer's cell phone rang. "That was the owner of the restaurant where Vlad eats lunch," she announced to the group. "The rain has flooded the road and he can't get the tour bus back up here. We'll need to spend the night."

"What?" Anna ran to one of the windows staring at the flashes of lightning. "We can't stay here. We must get back to the hotel." Her voice tinged with fear.

Rob gently embraced her. "It's all right. Don't be scared." He whispered in her ear. "I don't think this place is really haunted."

"It's not that." She shuddered. "I just hate the storm."

"I'm here with you and I won't let anything happen." Rob took her hand and led her back to the rest of the group.

"I've reached Mr. Campbell and he's assured me that we'll be quite comfortable here. There are guest rooms for the staff and the kitchen is well stocked." Jennifer smiled. "We will have to do our own cooking, though."

Several of the guests volunteered to fix dinner and they all went off to choose rooms for the night.

Rob and Anna found a small room along an inner wall without windows where Anna proclaimed she felt safe from the now raging storm outside. Going back downstairs, they joined the others for dinner. Sitting by the lit stone fireplace in the great hall, Jennifer told them more about Lord Erdely.

"No one has been able to trace where Lord Erdely came from before he lived in this castle. There are no records of his true date of birth, thought to be in 1624 and he reported to have died in 1654, but his body was never found. He simply disappeared one summer day after being seen heading toward Cornifu. Many people on these tours and several of the association staff have reported seeing the Lord roaming the stairs of the castle at night."

A flash of lightning lit the far end of the hall, and thunder roared right outside the castle.

Anna shivered when she felt a cold breath of air on her neck. Looking around she saw no one behind her.

She grasped Rob's hand. "I'm tired. Can we go up to bed now?" Her face paled as she stared at the shadows cast by the firelight at the end of the now darkened hall.

"Sure, hon." Rob stood, putting his arm around her shoulders as they headed for the stairs. "Good night, all. We'll see you in the morning. Maybe Vlad will be here with the bus."

Once in the room, Anna shrank from the door and perched on the edge of the bed shivering slightly.

Rob helped her undress and get under the covers, but she continued to shiver. He wrapped her in his arms. "The walls are so thick here that we shouldn't even hear the storm. We'll be able to leave in the morning." He gently rubbed her arms. "I'm sorry this turned out to be frightening. We'll head for Brasov as soon as we get back to the hotel."

* * * *

Anna sat up in bed, trying to see in the faint light spilling under the bottom of the heavy wooden door. She'd heard voices outside their room. Glancing at the illuminated face of her watch she noted it was three o'clock in the morning. Who would be out there?

"We need to be off early to town to fetch the eggs for his lordship. Ever since that wench from Brasov spent the night, the hens stopped laying," whispered a deep voice right outside the door. "I thought she had gone for good."

"I noted you enjoyed the sight of that wench. You should be pleased she has returned." A feminine voice answered. "His Lordship's women usually return."

Anna turned to Rob who was snoring lightly. Did he get one of the other couples to pretend to be Lord Erdely's servants to frighten her more? He wasn't that type. He had always been her protector. The voices faded and Anna snuggled against Rob's warm body and fell into a fitful sleep.

* * * *

"Jennifer, do you believe the castle is haunted?" Anna asked as they put a pot of water on for coffee.

"I've never seen the Lord or any others but I have felt a presence here. Several other guests on this and other tours have reported seeing Lord Erdely and even some of his servants." Jennifer smiled hesitantly. "Why do you ask? Did you see something last night?"

"No, but I thought I heard two people talking outside our room. They sounded like servants, but Rob has played tricks on me before and might have asked one of the couples to pose as Lord Erdely's servants." Anna poured herself a cup of coffee and offered the pot to Jennifer. "What I can't figure out, though, is if they *were* the servants they should have been speaking Romanian, yet I clearly understood what they were saying."

"Anna, I never saw Rob talking to any of the other guests when you weren't right by his side. On other tours, guests have seen the servants but not heard them speak." Jennifer poured herself a cup of coffee and the two women sat at the small table in the modern kitchen. "I know this situation is unsettling and I'm afraid I have more bad news for the group. The rain has started again and I called Mr. Campbell. The road is still awash. We may have to spend another night here."

Anna sprang from her chair, tipping it over. "No," she shouted. "I have to leave here. I can't stay any longer." She turned and fled the room running into Rob who stood in the doorway. "We have to leave. We can walk to the town." She grabbed his hand pulling him toward the door.

"Anna, if the bus can't make it up that road, we'd never be able to walk down. It isn't safe."

Her whole body trembled in his arms as he led her to the fireplace. Someone had stacked more logs on the fire and the warmth spread over them. "We'll be okay. I won't let anything hurt you."

As they entered the great hall Anna shivered as again she felt a puff of cold air on the back of her neck. The rest of the tour group had gathered for breakfast. Anna glanced at the second floor. Was that a flash of red behind the squint?

"Rob, someone's up there." She pointed to the narrow opening.

"Anna, we're all down here." Rob led her to the table. "You're just upset because we can't get back to town today. I promise we'll see the cathedral before we leave Romania."

After breakfast, several couples wandered around the other levels of the castle.

"Anna, let's explore the other towers." Rob smiled and turned toward the center staircase.

Anna reluctantly walked with Rob up the stairs. At the landing, she heard a whispered voice.

"I tell you she has returned." *The female voice from this morning.*

"Who said that?" Anna clung to Rob's arm.

"Who said what?" Rob asked. "I didn't hear anyone." He looked at his wife's pale face. "Are you okay? Maybe we should just stay downstairs by the fire."

"Yes, I'd like that." Anna answered and they headed back to the great hall.

The day seemed never-ending but the rain slowly stopped and some of the others went outside to view the destruction the storm caused.

Anna grabbed at Rob's arm when he rose from the bench they had dragged in front of the fire. "Please stay. Hold me, I'm scared."

Rob sank back down and held her in his arms. He had hoped this trip would bring them closer after Anna's uncharacteristic behavior following her return from Germany. Now he was concerned, his very independent wife acted like a frightened child. "I'll stay. Everything will be all right."

* * * *

The group spent a restless afternoon, exploring the smallest chambers in the castle and looking through some of the books the staff had in the tiny office off the updated kitchen.

They had dinner together and again sat in the great hall by the fire. Jennifer received a call from Bruce Campbell.

"It's supposed to dry out tomorrow and Mr. Campbell assured me they'll be able to get the bus through in the morning," she announced to the group. "I'm sorry that we have to spend another night here."

"Rob, I'm tired. Let's go to bed. The sooner we can leave here the better. I don't think I want to see another castle." Anna stood but when Rob didn't get up, she asked again. "Please come up to bed now."

"Hon, it's still early. I've found this great book about Brasov and I want to finish it tonight. Then when we get to the cathedral, I can be your expert tour guide. You go on and I'll be up in a bit."

Anna reluctantly headed up the stairs. She left the light on next to the bed and slid under the covers. She was on the verge of sleep when she heard the door open slightly. "I'm glad you came up early, Rob." She turned toward the door.

A stout man with dark wavy hair, wearing a red vest and black breeches, stood in the doorway brandishing a long sword.

"My lady has returned to me." He strode toward the bed.

* * * *

Rob and the others were startled by a piercing scream from upstairs. "My God! That's Anna." He raced up the stairs to their room and found her sitting up in bed, her breath ragged. He reached her side in two steps and swept her into his arms. "I'm here. You're okay."

"H…he was standing right there." Anna pointed to the doorway where Jennifer and several of the other men crowded the narrow hallway. "I saw Lord Erdely." Anna was shaking violently. "He had a sword and spoke to me."

Jennifer silently entered the room and moved to Anna's side. "Will she be all right?" she asked Rob who was slowly rocking his wife in his arms.

"I'm not sure. Do you think she really saw something?" Rob gently stroked Anna's shoulders and slowly felt her trembling diminish.

"He was right there." She squirmed out of Rob's arms. "You don't believe me."

"I'm not sure what to believe." He turned to Jennifer. "Have any of the ghosts spoken to people before?"

"I don't know. They might have. Often people don't report they've actually seen a ghost on the tour. Of course, we usually don't stay here past the late afternoon." Jennifer turned to the others in the hallway. "I think the Colliers would like to be alone. You can all go back downstairs or to your rooms for the night. We'll be leaving in the morning." She turned to Rob. "If you two are all right, I'll go downstairs, as well."

Rob nodded his head and watched her close the door. "Hon, are you okay now?" He kicked off his shoes and lay down next to Anna, bringing the blanket up to cover them.

"I just want to go home." Anna choked back tears and buried her face against his chest.

* * * *

The next morning, Rob rolled over and felt for Anna next to him. She wasn't in bed. *She must be feeling better*, he thought, before heading downstairs.

He found Jennifer sipping a cup of coffee in the kitchen. "I'm surprised my wife hasn't joined you. She's not really awake until her second cup of coffee." He laughed.

"I haven't seen Mrs. Collier this morning. I thought she was still upstairs with you," Jennifer answered. "I've called Mr. Campbell and he's assured me a bus will be here this morning to take us all back to the hotel."

Rob looked out the back door and noticed the sunlight streaming across the animal's pens. "Since it finally stopped raining, Anna must have gone outside for some fresh air. I'll tell her we'll be leaving soon." He headed outside.

After searching the grounds and the common rooms in the castle, Rob began to worry. He asked the others on the tour if they'd seen his wife, but nobody had since the night before when she claimed she had seen Lord Erdely's ghost.

Finally he headed back to the kitchen. "Jennifer, I'm getting worried about Anna. I can't find her anywhere in the castle or on the grounds. Something must have happened to her. I don't think she would have tried to go down to the town alone. She knew the bus would be coming back this morning."

"We've all been a little stir-crazy stuck here for two days so perhaps she went for a walk. It's quite nice out there now," Jennifer said. "You said your wife is an architect. There's a path along the woods that affords a nice view of the castle. She might have wanted a last look before we leave. Why don't you go out past the kitchen while I start around the front? We're bound to find her."

Rob quickly found the path along the edge of the woods. "Anna," he called. "Anna, are you out here?" He spotted a small clearing and when he reached it found a fenced-in cemetery. There, footprints in the wet ground led up a slight hill.

Rob followed the footprints around ancient headstones until they ended before a small granite marker covered in leaves.

He brushed the leaves off the marker. His legs suddenly felt leaden. It was difficult to breathe. "Anna Collier." He read aloud. The date of birth matched his wife's. The date of death was fourteen months ago. The exact time Anna had been on the trip to Germany.

"This can't be." He stumbled back toward the castle.

"Rob, wait." Anna appeared from behind one of the trees. "You can't tell anyone."

She moved to stand in front of him. "I didn't know why, but I knew we mustn't come here. I couldn't remember."

Rob drew away from her. "What are you talking about? What does that mean?" He pointed to the marker.

Anna turned toward the grave. "It's mine," she whispered.

"What the hell do you mean, it's yours?" He grabbed her shoulders and spun her around to face him.

"Th...there was an accident. I wanted to see you again. I can't go back now." She rambled on.

Rob's hands fell to his sides. "I don't understand." He stepped back. "You died?"

"Peter Gartner, one of the German architects told me about this town." Anna moved to a stone bench next to the fence. "I remember it now."

Rob sank down on the bench facing Anna. He reached toward her then pulled his hand back. "Remember what? This isn't real."

"It is Rob. I'm so sorry. I loved you so much." She looked toward one of the towers. "I took a train to Brasov. There's a small bus line to the town. I walked up the hill. No one was here. I took such wonderful pictures."

"No! Stop this. I don't believe you." Rob stood and headed toward the castle. "This is some sick joke."

Anna's hand felt cold on his arm. How had she gotten in front of him? He stopped, and stared into her soft hazel eyes filled with tears. "It's the truth?" he whispered.

"Yes," Anna replied. I remember it all now...

* * * *

Anna walked slowly around the gray stone walls of Lord Erdely's castle. The soaring towers and the narrow windows were just as Peter described them. "I'd love to see the inside."

She tried several doors but they were all locked. Walking around the pens in the yard, Anna pulled on the handle of the kitchen door and it slowly creaked open. She glanced around to be sure no one saw her slip into the castle.

The old kitchen was small with a huge fireplace dominating one entire wall. Two black kettles and a spit hung from an iron bar over several logs. She smelled wood smoke and it reminded her of visiting her grandparents' cabin in Vermont in the cold winter months. Her grandmother would cook stew in a kettle over the open flame.

Anna took several pictures of the kitchen and moved into the great hall. Long tables were set with crystal goblets that sparkled in the sunlight filtering through the larger windows.

"Is anyone here?" she whispered, afraid she'd hear an answer.

She was met with silence and shivered in the cold air.

Moving closer, Anna noticed the layer of dust on the table and benches.

She moved through the great hall and started up the stairs. She took a picture of the knight's armor on the landing and the carved door on one of the bedchambers. Reaching one of the towers, Anna pushed the door open and moved to the window. She could see the small town in the distance and the small graveyard below.

"Who has entered my home uninvited?" A deep voice echoed off the walls.

Anna looked, but couldn't see anyone else in the tower.

"Who's there?" she asked, moving back from the window.

"John Erdely, my lady," was the reply.

Anna spun around. A stout man with dark wavy hair wearing a red vest over a white shirt with billowing sleeves and black breeches stood in the doorway blocking her path.

"Okay, that isn't funny. I'm sorry I snuck inside." Anna laughed. "Are you getting ready for a reenactment? A banquet maybe?"

The man reached out and touched Anna's long hair. "You be a pretty young wench."

She shrunk back from his cold hand. "Wh...who are you?"

"I have told you, Lord John Erdely." His body seemed to flicker in front of her. "Now tell me your name."

Anna turned and tried to move past the man, but he grabbed her long hair and pulled her to him. Anna struggled but his arms were like steel bands holding her to his body. He smelled of sweat and liquor, his hands icy-cold.

"Now, a lady should not struggle so. I only wish to know your name." He stroked the side of her face with his right hand, his left tangled in her hair.

"Anna, my name is Anna." She tried to relax in his grip hoping he would release her. "Now, please let me go. I'll leave. I'll even leave my camera, see?" She held the little camera out in front of his face.

He smacked the camera from her hand. "It is you that I wish, not some trinket." He pulled a short sword from his waistband and sliced through her hair in one swift movement letting it fall to the floor. "Now no other will want you." He pushed her to the floor.

Anna screamed as the blade skimmed the back of her head. She scrambled to her feet and tried to reach the door.

He grabbed her again and Anna turned toward the window. Maybe someone would hear her yell for help. She stumbled and he appeared in front of her, but she could see the wall through his body.

He grabbed her arm once more. Pulling out of his grasp, Anna leaned against the window's edge.

"Help!" she screamed.

She felt his hands on her back and twisted away from him. The massive stone at the bottom of the opening shifted in the crumbling mortar and Anna felt herself falling. The impact on the ground was painful and she struggled to breathe. Anna sat up slowly, moving her arms and legs. "Nothing's broken, though I'll likely have bruises by morning."

Anna rose to her feet and peered at the tower window expecting Lord Erdely's face to stare down at her. No one was there. She ran to the front of the castle glancing back over her shoulder, sure she was followed.

Reaching the path, Anna felt her heartbeat slow and her stomach settle. It couldn't have been real. When she reached the town, Anna saw her reflection in a store window. Her hair barely reached her shoulders. It had happened! She sobbed in relief. She'd gotten away from the crazed ghost, but who would believe her? She'd always scoffed about Rob's belief in ghosts.

Clutching her waist-pack against her, Anna stumbled along the sidewalk. A small tourist office showed a bus schedule in the window. A bus to Brasov was leaving in less than an hour. She stopped at one of the small cafes for a soothing cup of tea and boarded the bus when it arrived. Back at the hotel, she entered the beauty shop, had her hair cut into a more attractive style and returned to Germany the next day.

* * * *

"I tried to put the whole episode behind me. I couldn't tell you about seeing a ghost after teasing you all these years. After a while I thought I'd just decided to get my hair cut short on the trip.

"I knew we shouldn't have come here. I didn't know why until this morning. I died that day, but I didn't want to leave you. I was able to come back to you."

Rob felt his heartbeat racing, his breathing ragged. "But your name is on the marker?"

"It isn't really there. You only see it because we're here. I should never have come. Now, I can't go back with you. I belong here now."

Taking one of his trembling hands in hers, she reached out and gently wiped the tears from his face. "You have to go on, Rob. Know that I always loved you." Anna leaned in and kissed him on the cheek, rose and moved toward the trees. "Goodbye, Rob."

He looked and she was gone. Rob stood in front of the marker again. The writing was in Romanian. He only recognized the single date—the date of death. He closed his eyes in grief.

* * * *

Coming down the path, Rob saw Jennifer enter the rear of the castle and he followed her into the kitchen. She was talking on her cell phone.

"Yes, they'll be very pleased. We'll be ready." She hung up and saw Rob. "That was Mr. Campbell; Vlad is on his way to pick us up." She noted his reddened eyes. "Are you all right, Mr. Collier? Did you find your wife?"

"Yes, she's outside." He mumbled. "I must be allergic to something out there." How could he possibly tell her what happened? "I found the cemetery. There's a newer grave there with only one date on the marker. Do you know anything about it?"

"That's a sad story," Jennifer answered. "Last year a woman's body was found by the trees. She appeared to have fallen from one of the towers. There was no identification and the locals, fearing the ghosts, buried her there. No one ever looked for her and there were no reports of anyone missing. They didn't tell the association until we discovered the grave."

"What does the marker read?" Rob asked in a shaky voice.

"'An unknown soul, may she rest in peace among the angels.' The single date is the date they found her body."

They heard the bus horn outside.

"That's Vlad. Now go and tell your wife we're leaving." Jennifer moved toward the great hall. "The others are waiting. I know we'll all be glad to get back to Cornifu."

"May we stay here a bit longer?" Rob asked. "We can walk down to the town and get the bus back to Cornifu. I understand there's a bus this afternoon."

"That's very unusual. I'm not sure if it's allowed."

"I can sign a release it that's needed. We just want to admire the outside of the castle. We couldn't enjoy the architecture in all the rain."

Jennifer pulled out her phone again. "Let me check with Mr. Campbell."

Rob waited in the kitchen doorway while Jennifer placed the call.

"It's all right with Mr. Campbell, he just wants a short note from you that it's all right to leave you and your wife here."

Rob signed the note and watched the bus turn onto the dirt road. He'd propped the back door open when Jennifer was speaking to the others in the group.

He reached inside his pocket and took out Jennifer's digital camera. He pushed the button and it still worked. He scrolled through several pictures of the castle grounds, the knight's armor and then a picture of the inside of the tower room. A hazy shadow filled the doorway although the light seemed to be coming from the opposite direction.

Rob pocketed the camera. He slowly walked back to the cemetery. Once again, he read Anna's name on the marker. He sank onto the bench, fresh tears coursing down his face. "Why, Anna? I need you."

"Go home, Rob," her voice whispered.

Looking up he saw the Romanian words on the marker. "Know that I'll always be with you in your heart."

Rob wiped his eyes, stood and started walking down the hill.

AUTHOR'S BIO: Carol Cole is a pediatric physical therapist and has worked for the past twenty-five years in a Virginia school system. Always a voracious reader, Carol began writing six years ago. Her stories have been published in over thirty-five online and print magazines. She has storied in two other anthologies, "By the Chimney With Care" and "Aleatory's Junction" She lives with her husband and twenty-one year old son, in Vienna, Virginia. She can be reached at http://www.carolacole.com.

Divine Curse
By
Kristin Johnson

"I told you, Jack, I'll never believe it," Ghillean said.

Jack was playful. "It is actually humanly possible to survive without Linux, Earp. For that matter, it's possible to survive without WebSphere, Google, C++, Firefox, 802.11—"

"Okay, Doc Genius," Ghillean said. "You try explaining that to the Emerging Technology Grant Committee that paid for our plane tickets to Bucharest and put us up in this…quaint…hotel with no Internet access."

Jack rolled his eyes. "You have your Blackberry, you don't need it. All I'm saying is, technology's overrated."

Ghillean "Earp" Morgan mock shuddered at slender, good-looking Jack "Doc" Onizuka. "You're Asian, isn't that some kind of Buddha blasphemy? They ought to kill you in the name of Sanyo."

"Seppuku on a memory stick? Hey, I'm a 'model minority' who slammed back too much Absolut and dropped out of Cal Tech. How many Japanese do you know who can boast about that?"

"None, but what do I know, I'm just a gai-jin."

"So am I, my sharpshooting friend. Actually, I'm a gay-jin. Nice hotel."

Ghillean laughed, as Jack intended. "Speaking of Absolut, where are those cocktails?" He waved at a red-uniformed server in the bar with the mammoth fireplace.

The red swatches everywhere added a hint of the forbidden to the Hotel Cornifu, as if the devil's fingernails that Romanians called the Carpathian Mountains didn't clue the tourists they were in another world. The fairy-tale high ceilings adorned a design straight out of a Gothic romance with the oppressively ornate heavy wood furniture and huge arched doorways as well as windows, the perfect frame for plucky orphaned paranormal-prone heroines and sinister sexy love interests, as well as insane housekeepers.

Jack fidgeted. Jack never fidgeted. He played with the lightning bolts of streaked blond and magenta in his glossy black Mr. Spock hairdo. It looked oddly out of place here in Gothicland, and the stone walls exuded a stiff, disapproving-grandmother feel.

"Uh, listen, project's ahead of schedule, right…"

"We could deploy another backup server, but basically…" Ghillean shrugged. "What do you have in mind? Touring Hunedoara Castle just for yucks?"

Jack's face was serious. "I wish you wouldn't—"

"You watch too many movies. You're probably thinking some creepy guy in a Boris Karloff reject costume will come and warn us not to go to Hunedoara. Then like in 'Hostel' after a round of sex…"

"Just because I'm gay doesn't main I want to jump you." Jack yanked a letter out of his pocket.

"I didn't mean with you, Doc, and I know you know I play for only one team—the Swedish Bikini Team."

"So you keep telling me. At least once a day."

Ghillean snatched the letter out of Jack's trembling fingers. "Besides, looks like you've got a love-letter from an admirer. Let's see what your latest toy boy has to say."

He pulled the vellum out of the envelope and read in disbelief. "This has got to be some freaking joke."

Jack shook his head mutely.

Ghillean stared at the gold lettering.

Dear Ghillean "Earp" Morgan and Jack "Doc" Onizuka:

We cordially invite you for a free tour within the famous castle of Lord Erdely.

Our guide, Jennifer Brooks, will be departing tomorrow at 8am sharp from Hotel Cornifu for this one day excursion we have planned.

Visit the mysterious surroundings of the Erdely Castle and see for yourself if it is indeed haunted.

Yours truly,
Bruce Campbell
President of The American Paranormal Association of World Tours

"You have one too," Jack said. "But in your steely-eyed gunslinger riding into town way, you ignored it."

"Give me a break, Doc." Ghillean took a swig of a tall glass of Vampyre Vodka. At least the staff in this burg had a sense of humor. "They just do that for the tourists. *American Paranormal?* Give me a freaking break. No wonder the rest of the world thinks we're nuts. Bruce Campbell? Is that even a real person or an 'Evil Dead' junkie?"

"Jennifer Brooks doesn't sound like Igor, either." Jack elbowed him. "Maybe you'll finally score, Earp, huh?"

Ghillean refused to rise to the bait. "I never even heard of this Lord Erdely. I heard of some woman, really whacked out, name something like that, who bathed in the blood of village maidens."

"Erszebet Bathory. Related to Vlad the Impaler. So you're closeted after all."

"Lit minor in college. Which I finished, by the way."

Jack grinned. Somehow, he seemed to enjoy the sparring. "So, are we on for eight tomorrow or are we going to be too exhausted from an amorous night?"

Ghillean stared at him with his best Wyatt Earp gaze. "8 a.m., pardner—this town ain't big enough for the both of us."

Jack laughed. "We can take one day out of our mission to bring fouled tech support and gibberish manuals to the impoverished. Now, that Vampyre Vodka looks tempting…and I'd like to sink my fangs into a nice…steak. Bwa-ha-ha. I am Dwacula!"

He did a convincing Bela Lugosi stare, and Ghillean and the crowd responded with shrieks and guffaws.

Mercifully, there was no old Gypsy in the room to predict their doom. Just regular international sensible-minded, party-minded tourists. And no Igor in sight.

* * * *

Jennifer Brooks most certainly did not resemble Igor. She was a stunner. Brunette with shoulder-length hair, a confident walk and a figure to die for. She wore no wedding band on the hand that held a clipboard. She checked off Ghillean and Jack as they gave her their names.

"So glad you both could join us." She smiled winningly as the bus driver, who did look like Igor crossed with Ben Stiller, ambled past, counting heads and twitching.

"Don't worry about Vlad, he's not crazy. He's reliable."

"Vlad?" Ghillean felt a jolt.

"Common enough name here." Her teeth sparkled. "He looks like an extra, doesn't he?"

"Can I ask him for his autograph?"

"He's deaf and he's never said a word on any of these tours. Are you goosebumped yet?"

"This whole thing is sort of Hollywoodish." Ghillean smiled. "And you are definitely star quality."

"Why, thank you. We all better get on the bus because the main attraction awaits, and the weather gets rough up in the mountains." She briskly moved on down the line of thrill-seekers. Ghillean silenced Jack with a look like hard spikes.

"But first," Jennifer continued, "Maya of the Gypsies will bless us, protecting us against the strigori—the vengeful spirits of the damned that Romanians believe haunt Castle Erdely."

A tall, rotund woman in a kerchief sprinkled everyone with holy water, burned some sort of incense, muttered Romany words and shooed them onto the bus.

Once Ghillean, Jack, and their fellow sightseers buckled in and were seated like first-graders, Jennifer stood in front of the bus.

"Good morning, everyone. For those of you who don't know, I'm Jennifer Brooks, a guide for the American Paranormal Association of World Tours. I'll be conducting your tour of Castle Erdely. Before we start, I'd like to answer some common questions.

"Number one: What is Castle Erdely? It's an ancestral castle that used to be an insane asylum. We purchased it from the Romanian government three years ago. Its original titled owner, Lord Erdely, vanished in 1654.""

She paused, grabbed the loudspeaker intercom, and sat as the bus made its ascent.

"Lord John Erdely lived in the 17th century. Rumor has it, although we don't have any documents or even anecdotal evidence to prove it, that he dealt in black magic to suppress the ongoing collaboration of the churches to bring a unified religion to all people—the Greek Orthodox Church. Lord Erdely was pretty famous for bodily throwing priests, missionaries and even an archbishop out of his castle. He was a card-carrying atheist.

"Local legend says he may have used black magic to contain his servants, to blind and deafen them from words spoken to them while on errands for the Lord within the village of Cornifu."

Ghillean and Jack glanced at Vlad and giggled like two rugrats.

Jennifer glared their way before continuing.

"Villagers became increasingly suspicious of Lord Erdely when their loved ones who were working for him didn't come home for visits. Lord Erdely was a closed book. No one ever found out so much as a birth certificate, or any family for that matter…or even a body. He was born in 1624, and he supposedly died in 1654."

"Supposedly?" Ghillean smirked.

Jennifer smiled sweetly. "Yes, or none of you would have signed up for this trip. Every paranormal expert and historian in Europe and around the world has tried to solve the riddle of Lord Erdely, and find his ghost.

"Next question: Is Castle Erdely haunted? Some say that Lord Erdely still lurks the corridors—there are a few staffers who won't stay in the building past sunset, although weird noises and cold spots have been felt everywhere and anywhere. Some people think Lord Erdely's victims walk the halls, unable to rest, full of vengeful hatred. Other people think Lord Erdely is still alive. Unlikely, but remember, we're in Transylvania. Who are we to say that he's not a vampire still inhabiting the castle?" She grinned.

"Here's a bigger question, Ms. Brooks." Ghillean raised his voice. "Did the Church make Erdely disappear in some kind of Salem-style inquisition?"

Several passengers muttered words to the effect of "How dare you."

Ghillean looked at Jack, who normally at these moments searched for a hole to hide in.

Jack focused on Jennifer, and said quietly, "Maybe they found out he was gay."

Jennifer Brooks remained calm. "There's no evidence the Church had anything to do with Lord Erdely's…bizarre disappearance. And as for his sexuality, we don't know. We know nothing about Lord Erdely." She smiled with chutzpah. "Maybe you two ghost hunters will discover what happened.

"A few ground rules before we start. The bus departs promptly at four-thirty this afternoon after a light dinner from our well-stocked kitchen. The castle has no staff, only a once a month maintenance crew, and I don't want to have to pry you out of iron maidens, so please use common sense. Although most of the castle is safe and intact…"

"Most?" echoed a woman.

"Like any other old building, there are places you don't want to wander into alone. Some areas have suffered damage due to age and unexplained environmental factors." Jennifer smiled. "Although this tour is free, donations to repair the castle won't be refused!"

"Pass the coffin," quipped Jack.

"Stay with the group at all times." Jennifer settled back in her seat. "And most important rule: if by chance you do discover Lord Erdely's fate or see his ghost, please tell the rest of us…we'll be in the bus."

Ghillean and Jack played along with the expected laughter. Ghillean reached for his Blackberry. Jack frowned at him. Ghillean showed him the display screen. "Don't worry, Doc—not making any calls today. I just want to take pictures of Lord Erdely."

Jack looked out the window.

"That was a joke," Ghillean said.

"Bet he was gay. We all know what goes on in my bedroom is a threat to civilization, especially the way the Church thinks."

"Thought you were a lector."

"I am, in a church that accepts me. I have no problem with God or crosses or Nativities. If this Erdely had a grudge against the Church, well, that was his right, but the Church controlled Europe and suppressed everybody—women and poor. If Erdely's ghost is still around, you can bet he's angry."

"If he's still around, he's a demon with serious issues who should just move on and accept a raw deal."

"You're one to talk." Jack stared at him. "You were going to call her—"

"I told you, the camera—"

"You had your thumb on 7 and Shift—speed dial."

"Maybe she just needs space—"

"She thinks you're gay—"

"Yeah, well, I think her shrink is a quack. I'm over her. Honestly. And you should talk, you haven't had a date since what's his name." Ghillean grinned. "Maybe Erdely will vamp you." He laughed hysterically at his own joke.

Jack laughed too. "He'll probably single you out. Vampires love repressed hypocrites."

"Want to know what I think happened to Erdely?"

Jack shook his head, but Ghillean continued. "I think he got fed up with the Church, the villagers' superstitions, the doom and gloom and everyone looking over your shoulder. I think he faked his own death, escaped to gay Paree, and lived out his days with the can-can girls or King Louis or whatever. Probably died an old man in Provence stomping grapes and milking a goat. Or drank too much absinthe at the opera."

"We'll see, won't we?" Jack playfully snapped Ghillean's gold chain. He pulled it out of Ghillean's Tommy Hilfiger open-necked shirt. "Lo, what have we here?"

Ghillean fingered the moonstone with an "E" monogrammed on it. "Gram Harry's good luck charm. No idea what the 'E' stands for. For some reason, it cuts down on tech hassles. Kind of like a St. Christopher medal." He made a move to tuck it back in.

Jack stopped him. "Leave it out. We'll need all the luck we can get."

Ghillean choked back laughter. Jack's serene face looked serious, like a kid saying there are monsters under the bed. Ghillean didn't know much about Jack's family, but Jack never talked to any of them except when they wanted help with their computers. Hell of a way to live.

Ghillean left the moonstone in plain view around his neck as Castle Erdely rose majestically beyond the windshield. The bus passed through a wrought-iron gate that slid open with an eerie dignified silence. The fence reflected in the windows looked as if it could stop all the Roman legions or Visigoths in history.

The bus braked and the motor went silent. The doors hissed open. Jennifer Brooks stood. "Welcome to Castle Erdely, folks."

Jack's face was one big sunbeam. "Let's go, my man!"

Ghillean gamely followed. It was only seven hours. He could stand seven hours. He pretended to be interested in the main entrance the size of an airplane hangar with paintings of Louis XVI, the Blood Countess, Marie Antoinette, Archduke Ferdinand, Mozart, Liszt, Chopin, Catherine de Medici, a replica of La Joconde (he wondered if anyone here had ever been found dead in the middle of a pentagram with cryptic messages carved into rigor mortis). In other words, a who's who of Europe. Wait, were those portraits of Einstein, Tycho Brahe, Sophia Brahe, Kepler, Charles Babbage—the inventor of the computer—and his lovely helper Countess Ada Lovelace?

Were they all winking at him? Probably laughing at his silly Americanness.

How many corridors were there in this place, anyway? Could someone get lost in here, led by the wailing specter of a beautiful woman in white?

Did that suit of armor just salute him?

Was that mist gliding up the large stone staircase that reminded him of the moving ones in Harry Potter?

He laughed hysterically, and was met with frowns from half of his companions, rolled eyes and guffaws from the other. At least now he knew who the sane ones were.

Doc looked hypnotized at the French chandelier with at least thirty graceful golden arms (a Gothic accident waiting to happen.) Ghillean figured his fellow skeptics and his sarcastic inner monologue would make this trip bearable.

* * * *

Two hours later, once the tour concluded, Ghillean's skin felt as though it would shake apart. He desperately wanted to leave this place. However, the storm refused to cooperate. The tourists were stuck in the ultimate "tourist trap".

The wind and rain howled as Ghillean and Jack peered down the drawbridge at the storm. Ghillean caught Jennifer's sleeve as she bustled past. Vlad, Igor or whatever his name was had disappeared. Rain slashed the bus.

"How long are we talking being stranded up here? You said we'd leave as soon as we could. That was an hour ago."

Jennifer's voice was mild. She was either brave or on Xanax. "These freak storms usually let up around midnight or so, but we've run into a warm air mass from the Black Sea and Mediterranean that caused a storm front moving over the Carpathians. Our weather equipment predicts we'll be bunking here for… three days."

"Three…?"

"Yes, until the roads dry out and the bus can safely make the dangerous descent into Cornifu."

"What do we do in the meantime?"

"What you came here to do. Investigate this castle and find out if it is haunted. I'll be leading small groups into some of the areas where people have experienced the most paranormal activity." Jennifer gave him a level stare. "Can you handle it?"

Don't think about it, don't think about it…

He probably hadn't seen anything. Or felt anything. Imagination. Right.

"Of course—sure, it'll be fun. Where do I bunk?"

She continued to stare. "Are you okay?" When he didn't answer, she lowered her voice. "The villagers think this is a fortress of pain and suffering. And we've uncovered…evidence of torture. Maybe not from Erdely, but from previous wars. Whatever you believe, please respect this place."

"Respect, no problem, do you happen to keep any Vampyre Vodka around?"

* * * *

Ghillean shuddered. Had to relax. Couldn't relax. As Jennifer showed them the bedrooms, he relived the tour.

Traveling up the staircase in broad daylight. Spiral staircase to the tower. No broad daylight there, silly cliché. Hands moving over his body. Snapping at Jack, "Cut it out, joker!"

Jack hadn't been touching him. Told him to "unclench." Take the stick out of his butt. Jack had said, "stake," and that's when Ghillean lost it.

Two tourists passed around the next corner, all of them queuing up like peasants or lemmings to the slaughter, and Ghillean couldn't breathe.

Heat blanketed his body, rubbing against him like fine silk and Italian leather. As insidiously as the sensation crept in, it was gone, and he was cold to the nerve. Not cold to the bone. Nerves hurt more than bones.

"There's…there's something weird up there." One of the male tourists, white-faced, pushed past everyone on the stairwell, nearly causing a massive accident and lawsuit.

"That's what you were hoping to see." Jack held Ghillean's shoulders to keep him from falling.

"He can't have you, pet, you're mine."

"I have chills all over my body," someone else yelled.

"Who said that?" Ghillean whispered.

"I did," a female tourist said. "It's c-cold, so cold…freezing…"

Jennifer Brooks appeared in their midst. "Central heating is a problem in these old drafty castles. If we all keep moving, the air will warm."

Ghillean forced himself to relax. "Anything spooky up there in the tower?"

"That depends on your definition." Jennifer's face was solemn. "Now come on, everyone stay together."

A few minutes later, the other tourists had settled down, but Ghillean, for the first time, had the fear of God.

Now he was going to spend two nights of hell here.

* * * *

"Remember, Earp, I'm right next door for two nights if your gun jams."

"That's comforting." Ghillean hadn't brought so much as a change of clothing.

Jack handed him a bottle of Vampyre Vodka. "Jennifer said you asked for this. Mind if I join you? We can just drink it straight out of the bottle."

"Why straight vodka? Why not straight blood? Did you know that Erszebet Bathory lived in Cachtice Castle, drained hundreds of Gypsy girls? She had a kid that was deformed and she just locked him away—like *she* wasn't the monster. They called her the Blood Countess. 'Oh, sorry about your life, but look, no crow's feet!' Sick. This is the kind of place you wanted to visit. I don't care what happened to John Erdely. I just want to get out of here and go back to the States."

Jack listened to his shellacking. "Usually people who swear they don't believe in anything end up converted."

Ghillean was silent.

"Aren't you just a little bored with your predictable life? We're here for two days and we're not going anywhere. Now either you accept it and make a fool of yourself exploring the castle like the rest of us or you sit here sulking over your vodka. Your choice."

Ghillean stretched out on the thin coverlet and put a pillow over his eyes. "I'll sleep on it."

"I'm going to round up some of our fellow adventurers and go exploring, then. See you later."

Ghillean mumbled a goodnight and tried to shut the freakish world out.

* * * *

So cold.

I'll warm you. I'm good at that.

You are an unbeliever, aren't you? No, don't scream, my piglet. I can rob you of speech. There. Silent.

Let your limbs relax. Do not struggle, it only increases the sensations. I can see your pain in your eyes, pain and delight.

Allow yourself to enjoy being controlled. Feel me in you. In your neck. Feel me tasting you. Just a taste, to spread the Divine Curse. You are so strong, you taste delicious and heady. Your blood is potent. Like your friend's, I imagine.

Feel what I do to the pressure points. I once required torture implements… metal…for that same effect. More powerful, this, do you not agree?

Fortuitous you are alone. I promised I would claim you and I have. But you will never know the mystery of this castle, will you? All you will know is submission. And desire. And hunger.

So warm now. My work is done. Pleasant, eh? Good night, Ghillean. Enjoy your last night's sleep.

* * * *

He dreamed he couldn't scream, that someone pressed on his chest, and he awoke to a hungry horny hung-over feeling. Damned bed. His neck throbbed. He felt as he did when he'd run the Relay for Life.

He heard screams. Not his own. Jack's?

He walked, rumpled like his clothes, to the door and peered out. Then he pushed past the four tourists outside the entrance to Jack's room.

His heart caught in his throat. "Aw, no, man, God, no."

Jack lay pallid white on the bed, eyes staring up, mouth in a slack grimace. His pupils dilated. He was naked.

"Aw, no, brother." Ghillean knelt by Jack and felt for a pulse. Tried mouth to mouth.

"Mr. Morgan…"

Ghillean pivoted his neck around, although he sensed Jennifer behind him. "Is there a doctor in this place?"

Jennifer's voice was calm. "I know this is going to be hard, but your boyfriend…"

"He's not…"

"He's dead," Jennifer said gently. "We checked. I have some EMT training."

"How do you know?"

"I've been trying to revive him, and you, for the last forty-five minutes."

"Then who the hell screamed?"

"The rest of the tour group." Jennifer glanced at the door. "I forgot to properly manage the crime scene."

He wondered if he'd ever be warm again. "He can't be dead. Why, God? What killed him?"

Jennifer pointed to a wound on Jack's neck. Ghillean leaned in to scrutinize.

"It looks like a hickey."

"Of course it is."

"I didn't put it there. He wasn't my boyfriend."

From the doorway, an English tourist snorted. "You Americans. Like it makes a bee's balls what you do in bed. You call us uptight."

"He wasn't my boyfriend."

Jennifer was calm. "Then who did he have sex with last night?" She nodded without a hint of diffidence toward Jack's genitals.

Ghillean didn't need "CSI" to see the evidence. He blushed, while Jennifer remained cool. He could see in her eyes the death had shaken her, but she remained calm for the tourists' sake. He had to admire that.

"I don't know. It wasn't me. I passed out blotto after seven, eight, maybe. He said he was going to explore with a group." Ghillean rubbed his throbbing shoulder.

Jennifer gave him a strange look. "What's that?" She ran a thumb over his neck and he winced. "Someone gave you a hickey too."

"Why, it was you, sweetheart, don't you remember?" He knew it was rude the minute he heard it echo.

Admirably, she remained calm. "Find your arm piece somewhere else, Mr. Morgan, because I really don't care about your sex life, and no one else in the world does, either. But your behavior is certainly suspicious."

"I'll say it is," the British male tourist shouted. "Skulking about like a sodding nonce at midnight. Or were you too drunk to remember wandering around alone?"

"A nonce?"

"You call it a sex offender. A perv."

Ghillean bristled. "This Yank wants to knock your British block off."

"All right, all right." Jennifer played referee. "Were you exploring the castle alone last night, Mr. Morgan?"

"No, I was completely passed out in bed. Jack…If you think for one minute I could…" Ghillean was overcome. Strong silent type, hell. He knelt and bawled like a baby.

How long he remained there he didn't know, but he stopped sobbing enough to hear Jennifer shut the British tourist out of the room after too much blatherskite.

He slowly rose and met Jennifer's concerned gaze. "You really have no idea what happened here?"

Ghillean shook his head. "I swear on my life."

Jennifer's voice was gentle. "I'm so sorry."

"We can't just…leave him here."

"Until we can drive down the mountain and tell the local constabulary…" Jennifer spread her hands. "We're trapped up here with a corpse and a murderer stalking these halls. Everyone goes about in pairs. We're on lockdown."

"Fine by me. I never wanted to come here."

"Why did you?"

Ghillean glanced at Jack.

Jennifer placed a hand on his shoulder. "I am sorry."

"I…me too. I didn't mean to…"

"It's okay. If you can't be a jerk at a time like this, when can you? Apology accepted."

He blew his nose. "'Nonce'?"

"What can I say, they're British." Jennifer studied him. "Is there anything… anything…you want to tell me? Did you see or hear anything yesterday?"

He didn't want to, but some sense of honor pulled at him. "In the stairway yesterday…I heard someone talking to me. 'He can't have you, pet, you're mine.' No one else heard anything."

"Is that all it said?"

"Uh-huh. And someone was touching me." At her look, he snorted. "Not Jack. He told me to take the stake out of my butt. He was always making jokes like that. But someone was doing heavy petting. And then I was hot all over, burning up. It went away, and I was freezing."

"You weren't the only one." Jennifer peered at his neck. "But only you and Mr. Onizuka have marks."

He touched it. Sure enough, a hickey, with two raised bumps. "Are there bats or spiders or snakes here?"

"All of the above, but none of them talk. And I'm no herpetologist, arachnologist, or up on desmodontidae—"

"What?"

"Vampire bats."

"I know something about bats. The British did a study last year on the size of a male bat's brains versus the size of his balls."

Jennifer laughed. It was the kind of laughter when something isn't that funny, but you need to laugh to break the tension. "Seriously?"

"What can I say, they're British." They both laughed now. Gallows humor.

"Jack found it hilarious. They concluded that the bigger the brain, the smaller the…Jack said it explained a lot. I told him I agreed." He laughed harder. "Not that I…"

Jennifer gave him a hug.

"So what does it mean?"

"The bats?"

"No…what I experienced."

"If your friend hadn't been murdered, I might say it was your imagination, just to get you thinking. But we can't rule anything out."

"I wish it was my imagination."

"Believe it or not, Mr. Morgan, I wish it was too."

"Earp."

"What?"

"Jack always called me Earp." He had moved apart from her. He suddenly wanted to be alone.

She smiled a little. "Why?"

"We both liked cowboy movies. I called him 'Doc.'" He sniffed. "They both fought at the OK Corral."

"I know. You have a gun with you now?"

He shook his head. "It won't stop a—"

"I do," Jennifer said. "And garlic, holy water, stakes. I don't know if they're effective or not…"

"Let's hope Anne Rice was wrong."

****

It doesn't matter if you have an army with you, pet, you'll never be safe. Or should I say, they *won't be safe? You bear my mark, I bear yours, and as for your friend…*

****

Ghillean stood at the foot of the tower staircase with Jennifer and two tourists. One of them was the belligerent British man. Ghillean ignored him. The other was a half-Italian, half-Greek nun and professor of art specializing in images of evil. She and Jennifer ascended first. Ghillean and the Brit just stared at each other, waiting for someone to blink first.

"Well, go ahead then," the Brit said. "You're so, I mean you Americans, are so eager to charge headlong where angels won't go."

"You mean like our horror movies?"

"No, I mean like your bloody military in Iraq, and now we're quagmired there, too. As if your former president was better than a tin-plated dictator—"

"Watch it, pal, U.S. Air Force."

"Oh, is that so? R.A.F. Mr. G.I. Joe, you go."

Ghillean strode forward. He owed it to Jack. God. If he'd gone exploring with Jack, if he'd stayed with him last night instead of sulking in pride…

But his blood tasted so delicious, didn't it? I took him exploring after all.

"What the bloody hell is THAT?" The Brit slammed into Ghillean, knocking them both against the wall. They clung to unlit torches, channeling Mel Brooks, not Mel Gibson.

"Sorry, mate," gasped the Brit, "but look."

Ghillean looked up and saw it.

Opaque mist was always a bad sign in haunted places. *This* opaque mist marched towards them, then stopped.

Mist wasn't supposed to suddenly sprout veins, red and purple glowing ones, and a thousand red eyes the size of berries. It looked like Satan's Christmas decoration.

The red eyes swirled, becoming slavering mouths. A sexual thrill went straight to his groin, but his body felt in deep freeze. His bullet-hard nipples could have burst from his chest and torn the mist to bits. If he wasn't squinched up against the wall hugging himself.

The phantasm blanked his brain, except for one thought.

"Oh my God, the women."

"They're twice as tough as us." But the Brit didn't sound sure at all.

"What's your name, anyway?" Jack forced himself to breathe. No, not Jack, Ghillean. He was going insane.

"Ralph, mate, pronounced Rafe like the fine thespian. And you?"

"Ghillean. But just call me Earp."

They were belly up together as if at a bar, and that tends to cut differences rather quickly.

"Right, Earp it is then. Your…your friend, what was his name?"

"Jack."

"Right. Well, in the name of Jack, then, whatever ghoul or monster you are, get out!"

Ghillean heard the Sister shouting Latin. The phantasm abruptly faded, leaving a glowing curtain.

"It's not gone, mate," Ralph whispered. "It's got our chits and it'll be back. Bloody fine heroes we are."

Ghillean and Ralph charged through the curtain, breaking through to the other side.

Once he got his bearings, Ghillean found himself in the Red Bedchamber that they'd visited yesterday. This was Erdely's bedchamber, heavily ornate with luxuries that looked…brand new, as if the entire contents of Sotheby's Evil Wizard Sale had been helicoptered in.

The nun spoke in rapid Italian.

Ghillean nudged Jennifer, who looked calm as ever. "What's she saying?"

"Sister Sofonio says there's an evil presence here. The…I think she said Dark Arts. Apparently she's a Harry Potter fan."

"Does that explain the decor?"

Jennifer shook her head. "We replaced all the original antiques with ones that looked suitably lordly."

"Does that include a waterbed?" Ghillean knelt beside the canopied bed. A mysterious puddle drenched the carpet. He sniffed it and gagged.

Jennifer coughed as she inhaled the stench. "That's…that's oil. Burning oil, and…and…it smells like a graveyard. Phew."

Sister Sofonio prayed fervently. Ghillean closed his eyes. At everyone's gasp, he opened them. The putrescence was gone.

"Maybe some people are right." At Jennifer's raised brow, Ghillean forced his voice. "Maybe Lord John Erdely is still alive. Or maybe…undead."

* * * *

The evening was tense, and no, not even the most devoted ghost hunters, or strigori hunters, wanted to go exploring.

The Gypsy's blessing hadn't worked.

Jennifer flitted in and out, doing a head count, "or a headless count," she joked darkly.

Ghillean's body felt like burning and cool sands all at once, like a deep freeze fighting a bonfire. He couldn't sit still, unlike last night. After Jennifer's head count, he crept into the corridor and stealthily made his way towards the staircase.

"Aha, skulking around at night again?"

"Bugger off," Ghillean told Ralph. "Isn't that what they say in your country? And what do you think you're doing…skulking about again?"

"Pursuing you, mate. You heard the lady tell us to sit tight, you did."

"I didn't hear anything of the kind."

Ralph slammed him against the wall, solid lean frame pinning him. "I bench 250 of your pounds, mate, and ghosts don't frighten me, not when the wankers I arrest walk free again. We're catching your American justice disease. The question is, why doesn't the ghost frighten you?"

"You think it doesn't?" Ghillean trembled. "I can't, I can't go back to my room. My…my friend died…I think…something is seducing me. That…that ghost, whatever it was…It felt like it's in me."

Ralph held him in place and studied his face. "I'm a lawman and I can tell when someone's lying…you're not. You really believe the ghost is inside you."

"I can't remember walking about at night last night. When you're possessed, don't you have blackouts?"

Ralph studied him. "Any other blackouts? 'Cos I'm not…I'm not entirely sure it was you."

Ghillean struggled against him. "Then, who…"

"I think it was that…whatever we saw…bedeviling us." Ralph crossed himself. "Sodding Godforsaken place."

"I haven't had any other blackouts. Just hearing voices from someone wanting to seduce me."

Ralph nodded thoughtfully. "Just hearing voices, is it? Well, that's a relief, since it's probably just you clawing your way out of that dungeon of respectability."

He gathered Ghillean in his arms.

Ghillean felt chills and heat, all over, sensitive, sensual, abraded, soothed, softening, hardening. He felt his manhood stir.

"I have to keep you under control, mate. Something weirdish is happening—something wicked. You can't be by yourself…don't blame you for not wanting to go back to your room."

"Don't trust me?"

Ralph smiled. He looked a bit like one of those actors from the modern British crime films, very rough and dangerous. He carried Ghillean, who was too drained to resist, to his bedroom. There, he eased them both down on a throne-like chair with clawed feet before Ghillean could inspect more of the décor.

Ralph kissed him, solid lean frame pinning him. Ghillean shrank away. He couldn't throw this man off, but…"Hey, hey, hey."

"Oh come on now, you're not starting that 'I'm not gay' again. Actually, I don't care if you are gay. I fancy you." Ralph kissed his neck. "I can't help it. I'm sorry about your mate, but life's for the living, eh?"

"You acted like…"

"Because I thought you were with him. Sorry I called you a nonce, after all. It's not as if I'm blameless…"

"I noticed you, and he got jealous." The words came hypnotically from his lips. "We, we had a falling out, Jack and I. It was my fault that…"

"No one's fault except the murderer's." Ralph rubbed up against him. "Your mate, he wouldn't want you to blame yourself. It's all right now, no tears, love."

"In danger…"

"I'm a bloody lawman, so I'll protect you."

"Please…"

"Oh, I'll definitely please. Since we're in Transylvania, don't mind, do you, if I nibble on you? Heh heh. You won't forget tonight."

* * * *

You little whore. This is the Divine Curse. It's exhilarating. Bring me what I crave.

* * * *

"What is that? Who is that?"

"Hmmm? Oh, you've got a hairy chest, I love that."

"I've been hearing voices since I got here."

"Really? Do tell more." Ralph sounded even more turned on. "Voices, you say?"

"A male voice…I heard it last night…in my dreams."

"Oh, and what is your dream lover saying now?"

"He…he says, 'he can't have you, pet, you're mine.'"

"Possessive little bugger."

He says, "'Fortuitous you are alone. I promised I would claim you and I have. But you will never know the mystery of this castle, will you? All you will know is submission. And desire. And hunger.'"

"Oh, tell me more…"

"'It doesn't matter if you have an army with you, pet, you'll never be safe. Or should I say they won't be safe? You bear my mark, I bear yours, and as for your friend…'"

Ralph jerked away from him. "You're having me on."

"No…I'm not." He saw the suspicion in those Westminster-gray eyes, the same color as the cropped hair.

Ralph shivered. "Bloody freezing in here, maybe we should get naked and good old body heat…"

"Do you want to know the rest of what he says?" Ghillean nibbled at Ralph's whip-lean muscles.

"Well, I don't..."

"Yes, you do." Ghillean stared hypnotically at him. "Yes, you do, or I stop this..." He flicked a nail over the muscle and Ralph moaned.

"Oh...tell, tell..."

"Why tell, when I can show you..."

Ghillean moistened the skin of Ralph's neck with his tongue, preparing it. Sensitizing it. Over-sensitizing it. Priming him to feel the contact to the ultimate.

"You abominable little tease."

Swiftly, Ghillean buried his new fangs, which thankfully, Ralph hadn't noticed, into the peat-smelling flesh. He pushed himself in to the hilt. Warm, resistant at first, yielding now. He drank, and drank, and drank.

He drank the memories from Ralph's life. An old vampire saying somehow floated in his mind: "Blood is the only reliable memory we carry—our pain and our sorrows are imprinted there."

Blood...blood...Ralph's grandfather insane...fighting his father in a drunken rage...how could you marry that little twat and now she's gone and left you with the brat...and he's not right...Ralph's grandfather killing his father and Ralph, barely eight, beating his grandfather senseless.

This excited Ghillean. He had to have more.

Ralph, in a home for boys...sullen and fighting...kicked out...taking to the streets, selling his body to Arab and Turkish businessmen, Greek nationals and Russians as well as British and Americans out for cheap thrills. Ralph busted by a British undercover bobby who then let him off after Ralph got him off. Ralph overdosing at fifteen. Found by a Kurdish refugee and her Christian missionary husband. Taken in, straightened out.

Knew he was gay early on. What was the bloody deal in the States with the age thing. He looked older anyway. Couldn't find it in him to hate the men who'd used him, but wanted love. Didn't have sex again until he was twenty-five and found a good man from Edinburgh. Together for ten years, Duncan got killed, traffic accident. Another dry spell of mourning. Vowed he'd never do that again. So hard at forty now to find men. Good men. Found a man in Ghillean. If he was who he said. Suspected him, wanted him too. Yank was eating him...wanted to kill...but so so delicious to be consumed...been consumed and used all his life...bloody fitting epitaph...orgasm in the blood.

Just as Jack experienced.

Ghillean was no longer sure if that was his thought or the demon's... whoever the demon was...perhaps they had merged.

Ralph's bloodless corpse sprawled over the chair. His head flung back in a grimace of ecstasy. His pupils dilated. And oh yes, he'd finished just like Jack. The last thing he'd known was surrender.

Ghillean wiped his lips with the moldering curtains. A spasm like epilepsy seized him and he fell prostrate, his forehead knocking against the ancient marble floor.

He jerked his head up as though God had seized him by the scruff of his neck and yanked him by the short hairs.

"What have I done?"

Disheveled, clothing in disarray, he slugged back the rest of the tea.

The corridors were empty, everyone presumably cubbyholed away, Jennifer still counting heads. He had to find her. He needed to tell her. Needed to throw himself on her mercy.

He stalked the corridor. His eyesight sharpened and he could see through the darkness with the wan light of modern electricity that dimmed progressively. But his new senses failed as he crossed into the tenebrous part of the hall. Deepest darkness. He put a foot out and plummeted as the antiquated stones collapsed beneath him.

* * * *

"Earp!"

Jennifer's voice revived him. Every bone in his body felt as friable as the stone and dust supporting his aching carcass. He slowly pulled himself up and stared through the gaping hole in the ceiling. Jennifer peered through. She was a welcome sight.

"Thank God. What the hell were you thinking? No, don't answer that. Are you all right?"

"No." It was the simplest answer.

Someone grabbed her around the waist and lowered her. He couldn't see her helper, but Jennifer grabbed him under the shoulders.

"In your spare time you do Krav Maga, right?"

"As a matter of fact..." Jennifer glanced up. "Let's try it, Hugh. Hold on tight, Earp."

He grasped on to her shoulders, her arms. She was stronger than she looked. He let himself go weightless as Hugh strained to pull them both up in a human cranehook.

How he made it out of that pit he didn't know. He didn't remember being moved. He sat in one of the offices as Jennifer and another tour companion, a woman doctor, examined him. "I don't believe it," the doctor said.

"That I'm alive?"

"That you don't have any broken bones after a fall like that. Your guardian angel must have shielded you." The doctor popped a Tylenol-3 in his mouth. "This will make you groggy, and I hope, keep you out of trouble until we can leave this cursed shithole."

Jennifer's voice was even. "What were you doing wandering alone when I specifically said you shouldn't be?"

Ghillean gave her the hypnotic gaze. "Lord John Erdely attacked Ralph."

"Ralph?"

"The Englishman."

"Oh yes, you two have..." Jennifer sucked in a breath. "Hold up. You saw John Erdely?"

"Felt him. Heard his voice." Careful now. "I think I've been hearing it since the stairwell yesterday. I was…um…okay, I am gay…"

"I know that. What happened?"

"He…he was trying to console me…actually he was trying to kiss me. Men, you know…Suddenly he just…I felt this surge of hatred and evil…I scrambled to get us away…I got away, but Ralph didn't…I felt Erdely pass right through me, and it was…he wanted to hurt me. I fled…I heard his voice taunting me. In my mind."

Jennifer looked skeptical.

"Go look in Ralph's room. I…I tried to give him some dignity. I…put him back on the chair."

"Before you ran from Erdely?"

"You do strange things when you've seen two people dead, naked, in less than two days."

Jennifer considered. "So you think Erdely attacked you while you slept, then…killed…your friend, and now went after Ralph? Why didn't he finish you off?"

"Startled him, I guess."

"Why did he pick you first?"

"Because I'm an unbeliever?"

"Ralph and Doc were believers. Why pick them?"

"To hurt me for not buying the Erdely curse? To demonstrate that he still rules? Why not pick a guy who's…" He swallowed. "Who was closeted? Who doesn't believe in the boogeyman because he's too busy being afraid of himself? He can sense fear."

"Is he in the room with us now?"

He couldn't believe she bought it. "No. I don't know where he went, but I bet he's still around."

Jennifer exhaled. "All right. I radioed for help. The storm front is dissipating. It should be all clear in the morning. When it is, we leave immediately. Until then, everyone gather in the Great Hall of the castle. No one, and I mean it this time, no one goes off alone. If you don't listen, you could end up dead. I've asked for a Gypsy to come and make sure Erdely, or whatever is in here, doesn't follow us."

"Where'd you find a Gypsy?"

"Remember Maya? Before our three-hour tour started?"

"Does she have a flying carpet or a broom?"

"Her Gypsy camp is halfway down the mountain, I sent one of your tour companions to find it so she can arrive and break the curse."

* * * *

The stalwart volunteer Jennifer sent out did not return. Jennifer refused to risk anyone else, had there been any takers. Everyone nominated Ghillean to perform a Gypsy ritual while Sister Maria Sofia Sofonio called on the Lord to do battle with the evil. Ghillean caught her muttering "Lumos" and other Latin phrases from Harry Potter.

They gathered in the chapel. Why an atheist like Lord Erdely had a chapel was anyone's guess, but all these older castles had them.

Ghillean beseeched the religious icons of saints, especially Jude, Christopher, Ursula, Teresa, Sophia, and Anthony, as well as local martyrs. *Help me believe. Help me have faith.*

After Sister Sofonio performed an exorcism, Ghillean mixed river water with seven coals, seven handfuls of meal, and seven cloves of garlic. He dropped them all in a fire pit, stirred the fragrant smoking burning mass with a three-forked stick, and recited a Romany chant.

"Miseç' yakhá tut dikhen,
Te yon káthe mudáren
Te átunci eftá coká
Te çaven miseçe yakhá;
Miseç' yakhá tut dikhen,
Te yon káthe mudáren
But práhestár e yakhá
Atunci kores th'ávená;
Miseç' yakhá tut dikhen
Te yon káthe mudáren
Pçábuvená pçábuvená
Andre develeskero yakhá!"[1]

He chanted in English for good measure:

"Evil eyes look on thee,
May they here extinguished be
And then seven ravens
Pluck out the evil eyes
Evil eyes (now) look on thee.
May they soon extinguished be!
Much dust in the eyes,
Thence may they become blind,
Evil eyes now look on thee;
May they soon extinguished be!
May they burn, may they burn
In the fire of God!"[2]

As the rite concluded, Ghillean felt more powerful and enervated simultaneously. Maybe the dreadful thing that had possessed him was gone…

The dreadful thing that had made him kill.

---

[1] http://www.magick7.com/gypsy-sorcery/moon-worship.htm

[2] http://www.magick7.com/gypsy-sorcery/moon-worship.htm

He blacked out again.

* * * *

He awoke again. The voice was silent. He had a throbbing headache and by rights he ought to be dead.

Jennifer sat by him in the Great Hall. The others cast frightened looks and whispers at him. The nun led them in prayer. He smiled weakly at Jennifer.

"You look like the undead stuck in the microwave for twelve hours."

"I'll live."

Jennifer admired Gram Harry's charm. "That's beautiful. Is it an heirloom?"

"My Gram Harry."

"Why does it have an 'E' engraved?"

"His name was Emilian, but everyone called him Harry because like me, he had a hairy chest."

"Emilian is a Romany name."

"I'm one-quarter Gypsy."

"You never mentioned that."

"Because I got sick of people asking for palm readings and voodoo spells. When your first name is Ghillean and kids already think you're weird…"

"Ironic, considering you've been bitten by a vampire."

"I'm not a bat, am I?"

Jennifer gasped. "Your hickey. It's gone."

He felt the juncture of his puncture. Smooth skin.

"How is that possible?" She scooted away from him.

"I'm a fast healer. Always have been."

He saw the resolve in her eyes, the realization. "No one could have survived that fall intact. But why haven't you tried to drain me? I thought you wanted me."

Somehow, he had the wisdom of blood. "You're protected somehow. I don't know how or why, but you are."

"If you're…if you're…you should have been banished when we did the ritual." Her voice was steady. "Is John Erdely alive?"

"I'll never tell." He lazily uncurled himself and rose over her. "I admire your courage."

"You don't know, do you?"

"Doc was right. He probably was killed because he was gay. I've survived a lot in my life, thanks to Gram Harry's black magic blood. And this talisman. It protects me. Takes a Gypsy to fight a Gypsy."

"You're an unbeliever…"

"Who better to carry on the family curse? And who better to feed it than believers?"

She glanced at the others, who devoutly, fervently prayed with the Sister.

"They can't hear us." He smiled. He felt powerful for the only time in his life. "Shall I tell you which ones I'm going to feed from?"

"I'll stop you."

"I may not be able to bite you, sweetheart, but I can deal you a world of hurt. And then I'll feed on the believers. Gay, straight, male, female, good, evil, it doesn't matter."

Uncharacteristically, she had nothing to say to this. He smiled again, kissed her on the lips before she could move, and swaggered off.

The Sister continued praying. Maybe it would save them. Let them believe. It was good to have a belief.

* * * *

His bones woke him with their screams.

He was in darkness, beneath the collapsed ceiling, chained to the wall without any chains. His eyes had gone completely blind.

"Who the hell dares?"

He heard soft laughter. Not inside his head. Outside. Male laughter.

"Doc?"

More laughter. He reached for the talisman. Nothing.

"You won't find it, you nonce." Ralph's voice. "Suspected you from the start, I did."

"You're…you're dead."

"Not so much. Now Doc and me, we're owing you repayment for our nights of passion. But we never did finish ours, did we?"

He felt lips and sharp teeth nibbling on his mouth. Doc's. Warm and sweet.

At the other end of him, Ralph's mouth worked busily. The kiss of pain. Licks like needles on his legs.

"What was it he said to you, love? 'Feel what I do to the pressure points. I once required torture implements…metal…for that same effect. More powerful, this, do you not agree?'"

Ghillean groaned.

"We know everything you know." Doc tormented his lips, his flesh, and his upper arms. "And I ought to have had you first, before anyone. You put me off with your disbelief. Now, I'm taking what you offered so teasingly."

Doc pushed his thighs apart, and then his whole awareness fogged out in a Tylenol haze. The damn drug finally worked.

* * * *

Torture was easy. All you had to do was make the subject love you. Start with what he secretly needs, and give it to him until he can't bear any more.

* * * *

Shadows. So many shadows. The aroma of meat on a spit. The scent of wine poured over the skin of a chained maiden, a chained pleasure-boy.

The rustle of a Romanian priest's robes. The sweat of his desperation and his prayer. The tang of his blood. A rat gnawing on his ear.

Shadows. A chained maiden forced to drink her own blood as her captor's semen mixed with wine spilled down her chin. A pleasure-boy kneeling between her thighs as demons used his body for their infernal pleasures.

The priest stretched out, his heart cut from his still living body with a crucifix to chew on.

Frenzied Romany violins and thousands of dancing feet just before fire consumed them at a ball.

The Gypsy exorcism mixture in the air, taunting.

* * * *

Ghillean woke once more, this time to the brutal invasion of his mind. Rape of his body he could have withstood, but his mind…his thoughts…He couldn't tell who was talking. Not the same voice taunting him.

Him: *I gave you, I gave you immortal eternal pleasure.*

A chorus: *No one ever said you'd receive it in return. You didn't give it freely.*

Him: *I didn't give myself freely either, I was taken!*

Chorus: *Adored, adored, adored. But you have no right to expect more, more, more. You have the Divine Curse and that is enough. Anything else you receive at our grace.*

Him: *Grace? You talk of grace?*

Chorus: *Cursed grace. Now, we're hungry again. You'll surrender now.*

Him: *I'll destroy you.*

Chorus: *Oh, but you were a naughty boy. Jack knows you. Always one to cheat, cheat on games, cheat on codes, steal inspiration. Always one to hide from your parents and then drink and complain they didn't understand you. Hiding behind charity to assuage your precious guilt. How you love the guilt, it's who you are.*

Him: *Get out of my mind. I'm…I'm dying. I can't give you anything more than me burning like a whore in hell.*

Chorus: *If you were a whore, you wouldn't go to hell. And you won't burn. We won't let hell have you. Anyway, it's all here on earth. We'll just keep you in this castle. See? Ceiling is all sealed, isn't it?*

Him: *You can't keep me here. They'll look for me.*

Chorus: *Doubt that. You see, everyone saw you attack Jennifer Brooks like a common criminal. She disarmed you. Everyone piled on you. Then, your injuries mysteriously surfaced and you ruptured internally. But of course you're not dead, though they all think you are. They've concluded you're the killer. They've all left this place. It's dawn, you see.*

Him: *Yes…the sun…Oh God, it's searing my eyes…*

Chorus: *There you go, the mask is back on. Blind again.*

Him: *Thank you.*

Chorus: *Blood from a rat?*

Him: *Yes, please.*

Chorus: *We have some prime human type AB stashed away. Until the tour company says this place is safe, you'll live on that.*

Him: *Jennifer knows I'm a vampire.*

Chorus: *Now, we fixed that. Your conversation with her took place in your mind, she thinks the Gypsy ritual banished the darkness. You confessed to killing both men out of self-loathing. You then perished. Word won't get out, no one will speak of it. The tours will continue. This time with an added attraction for the unbelievers. You do believe now, don't you?*

Him: Unfathomable excruciating scream.

Chorus: *You believe. If we think you believe, we'll grant you time on the office computers, won't that be nice?*

Him: *No computers, I believe, I believe, I believe…*

Chorus: *No computers?*

Him: *I believe, I believe, I believe…*

AUTHOR'S BIO: Kristin Johnson is the author of the Midwest Book Review 'enthusiastically recommended CHRISTMAS COOKIES ARE FOR GIVING (Tyr Publishing, 2003), co-written with Mimi Cummins. ORDINARY MIRACLES: My Incredible Spiritual, Artistic and Scientific Journey, written by Sir Rupert A.L. Perrin, M.D. with Kristin Johnson, was published by PublishAmerica in 2004. Ms. Johnson is also the author of BUTTERFLY WINGS: A Love Story (iUniverse, 2000).

Most recently she has delved into horror, both in the MuseItUpClub anthology ALEATORY'S JUNCTION as well as in the Summer 2007 issue of THE MAGAZINE OF UNBELIEVABLE STORIES. Horror kicked her screenwriting into high adrenaline mode. On a lark and on request from a producer, she wrote the screenplays that became the direct to DVD B-movies "Blood Mask" and "Pirates of Ghost Island". "Blood Mask" director Dennis Devine raves, "Kristin has the unique blend of poetry and low-budget horror styling that gives the genre a fresh twist." "Pirates of Ghost Island" was distributed by Lionsgate Films. She has completed a comedic murder mystery script adaptation, an animation series pilot, and several other projects. She is a ghostwriter and script consultant who is much in demand.

Ms. Johnson is an award-winning writer (1999 Edward W. Moses Graduate Grant in Creative Writing for "Sinatra's Dogs"; First Prize, 1997 3rd Tri-Annual Blue Mountain Arts Poetry Competition for "On Our Wedding: Ahava"; 2000 12th Tri-Annual Blue Mountain Arts Poetry Competition for "Wedding Dance").

A graduate of the University of Southern California Master of Professional Writing Program, she is the former First Vice-President of the Palm Springs Branch of the National League of American Pen Women (NLAPW) and former Vice-President of the NLAPW Southern California State Association. She's a member of Women in Film and the Original Palm Springs Writers Guild.

Ms. Johnson currently lives and writes in Palm Desert, California.

By the Light Of the Moon...

By

Kevin R. Tipple

"Is he here?"

"Yes, Commander."

"How is he?"

What he was asking was whether or not the suspect had made it alive into his station. He should have, but sometimes accidents happened in the field.

The young officer stepped a little ways into the room. New to his job he was working hard to impress—which is why the Commander had chosen him. Things had to be contained and he knew he could keep the man, more like a boy at twenty, in line.

"Typical American." The young officer couldn't keep the scorn out of his voice, "Very emotional. Fits of screaming and crying when we placed the cuffs on him. He's sitting quietly in Interrogation 4 now."

"Good. That will be all."

The young man saluted, swiveled in his black spit polished boots and strode confidently out of the office. The Commander sat back and smiled to himself while he listened to the pleasurable sound of the boots striking the floor fade away down the long hall. To be young again and so sure of righteousness, of purpose. Not that it really mattered as fate ordained everything. *His die was cast long ago as was my own*, he thought, and the idea depressed him as it had the last few months.

He stood and stretched, feeling his spine pop before he walked down the same hall. Unlike the young man before him who had turned right so that he could pass the front desk and go back out on patrol, the Commander turned left. After a few steps, he felt as if the walls were closing in on him.

The truth was they were as he journeyed deeper into the old section of the garrison. This part had been built into the mountain long ago and the Commander secretly suspected that there had to be a tunnel from here up to the castle far above. He suspected it but had never tried to find out because he knew that in such matters, a lack of knowledge was safer than the truth.

The back half of the garrison was a place the public didn't ever want to see. It was a relic of the past and the walls held in the cold and damp year round. Cinderblock walls that were conducive to putting the prisoners that found themselves back here in the right frame of mind. Gray walls that seemed to talk to him when he wandered around late at night, smoking his pipe, and contemplating the strange turn of events that had led him to this point. It was when he stood; smoking and contemplating his ultimate fate that he heard the screams of the past.

Upon reaching Interrogation Room 4, he popped the lock and swung the heavy steel door back with a strong pull. He let go as it moved, anticipating with a certain amount of relish the sound it would make when it crashed back against the wall.

The boom rolled through the area and down the hall and inspired the suspect to jerk upright in his seat.

Off balance from the start was always best.

The Commander stepped inside and gently pulled the door shut with a barely audible click. He stood there for a moment, allowing him to inspect the suspect before he interviewed him. Not that it ultimately mattered anyway—his fate had already been determined.

The suspect was about twenty years old, six foot or so and probably around 150 pounds. Lean and wiry, his dark and rather bloodshot eyes flicked nervously back and forth. The Commander smelled the stink of fear on him.

He was desperately in need of a shower. He sported a ridiculous goatee that needed to be shaved off immediately as it made him look more like a cartoon character than anything else. The Commander had an almost insane urge to tell him to go wash behind his ears and just managed to stop himself.

"I want a lawyer." The suspect leaned forward and said it again slowly and with exaggerated pronunciation as if the Commander didn't understand English as well as seven other languages. "I want a lawyer."

"No."

"But—"

The Commander sat down and stared hard at the suspect. It was best to get suspects in the right frame of mind from the beginning.

"You are a guest in my country. As our guest, you have no rights."

"I'm an American citizen."

When the Commander only raised an eyebrow in reply the suspect added, "I demand to see the American Consulate."

"There is no American Consulate. You would know that if you had studied your history or anything about the country you decided to grace with your presence. I have your passport, your records, your very life in my hands. I can dispose of you any way I wish with no one the wiser."

Not exactly true he thought to himself but there was no need for the now very red faced American to know the full truth. That would come soon enough. He rocked his head from side to side, trying to loosen the tightness in his neck. When this matter was over he had to go spend some time with Lida. Her healing touch was like magic to his body and what she could do in the bedroom was an added bonus.

He shook his head one final time trying to get back on track though he hated this aspect of his job most of all. Interrogations when the outcome was not already known he enjoyed immensely. The thrill of the hunt, the chase, the capture all got his juices going. A robot could do his job today and it gave him no satisfaction. Yet, he had made a bargain and failure to follow through on his end would have grave repercussions.

"You Americans think the world is your playground. What you don't blow up, you party in like it's yours. In both cases you throw money at the people involved to make amends. You make wars for no reason and think that everyone must be like you, think like you, and worship you. You haven't contaminated my country with your godless influences and won't because my people respect tradition and culture."

The Commander realized his voice had been steadily rising and he had been nearly screaming at the shaken American. He never had to scream again in his life and certainly not in this room. It was time to move on, so in a more gentle tone he said, "Now that you know your place, tell me what happened."

The Commander sat back and lit his pipe. He wouldn't need an ashtray for his pipe anytime soon and he could sense that he wouldn't need it because the American wasn't going to last that long. Another quick glance from his pipe at him revealed that the suspect was sweating profusely now and his face had gone very pale. The room was working to his advantage, as it always did, and the Commander puffed his pipe in satisfaction. This wouldn't take long at all. It never did.

"I don't know what happened."

The Commander blew a small perfectly formed smoke ring toward the small incandescent bulb in the ceiling. It hit and then drifted to one side where by the time it got to the twin hanging meat hooks it all but disappeared. The hooks twitched once, anticipating their use.

"Start with explaining how you had human blood on your hands. Did it come from Raquel?"

The young man swallowed hard and stared at his shaking hands.

"Where is she?"

"You tell me."

"Is she okay?"

The Commander said nothing. He sat and puffed on his pipe and allowed the American to stew in his own juices. Raquel had done her duty and moved on and that was the Commander needed to know.

"Man, you have got to tell me. I'm dying here."

How ironic.

"Go back to the beginning and tell me what happened."

The lanky American sat back with a sigh and a small shake of his head.

He was so close, it wouldn't take much more. The Commander used that extra little touch with his voice as he made the suggestion once more. "Start from the beginning and we will figure it out together."

"I met Raquel in Paris. It was just supposed to be a one night stand." He pulled a wry smile and looked up from the wooden table into the Commander's gray eyes. "You know what I'm talking about? One night stand?"

The Commander nodded and sent another smoke ring to the ceiling. "But, I fell for her. She got her hooks in, you know."

The Commander nodded again and it seemed like the suspect relaxed a little.

"I mean.... you know... she was beautiful and all that, but there was more to her. She was smart, too, and didn't flaunt it. I knew she was smarter than me."

Of course she was, the Commander thought.

"And she was fun. She had plenty of money but wasn't nasty about it. I was broke when we met in that bus station in Paris. I'd called home but my old man was being an asshole again. "No school, no money" he kept saying. I'd spent my money backpacking this far and I wasn't ready to go home."

He sighed and they sat there in silence. Once the suspect was talking it was better to let him keep talking at his own pace.

After a few minutes it became clear that he wasn't going to talk so the Commander prodded a little.

"So, whose idea was it to grace our lovely countryside with your presence?"

"It was Raquel's. She showed me some invitation deal to this stupid old castle."

"That stupid old castle as you put it was home to the family of Lord John Erdely. It is because of him that the village of Cornifu has survived the ages and continues to stand today."

The point was clear and the young man, as best as he had been taught, apologized. They moved on.

"So, Raquel had this invitation from some group that into magic and stuff to take some tour deal."

"Are you a believer?"

"No, man, that's all bogus crap." He paused for a moment, "Well, I wasn't. I don't know now."

Maybe he wasn't hopeless. Too bad.

"So, she had this invitation or something and she wanted to go bad. We took the train and came up a couple of days ago just when the weather got bad. We had to stand round and wait at the train station until this tourist bus pulled up. That guy was a trip, man. Weird as all hell with his weird eyes but he never said a word."

"That would be Vlad."

"I guess."

"The Securitate, many years ago, drove spikes into his ears to make their point."

The young man blanched and swallowed.

"He came back to the village of his birth to die but he survived. You would do well to learn his kind of courage."

His pipe had gone out so he let those words hang in the room while he emptied the remnants onto the floor and repacked his pipe. That was another nice thing about the old rooms. Water and everything flowed down the drain in the center of the room. It really didn't matter what it was. If something didn't wash down easily, there was always plenty of free labor for cleaning duty.

Once the pipe was going again the Commander gestured for him to continue.

"So, we and a bunch of other people got on the bus."

"Do you know who they were?"

"No, man, I think they were all Canadians. Heck, everything north of the Red River is Canada anyway."

He laughed and then quickly stopped when the Commander didn't join in.

"See, that was a joke. Texas is…"

"I know exactly where Texas is. In my country, you don't do my job without a lot of education. I speak seven languages and you can barely speak your own."

The Commander had to reign in his temper. The suspect's ignorance knew no bounds.

"I really wasn't paying attention to anybody else. I remember our tour leader or something. Her name was Jennifer and she was pretty hot. She took it all real serious though."

"Took what seriously?"

"Her lecture on this dude that lived way back when in the castle. She went on and on while that bus went up the side of that mountain. It was lightening and thundering and in the back of the bus we could see over the side down the mountain when the bus made a turn. I even said to Raquel it was something out of a movie and she just smiled and kissed me. Pretty much lost track of everything at that point. I mean I knew that magic voodoo stuff was bogus. I just wanted to be with Raquel and I was. We finally get up to the castle. It was pouring like crazy and really dark though it was ten in the morning or something. They take us inside and give us a tour of the place. After that they fed us and that was okay."

The Commander nodded and puffed on his pipe a little more.

"After lunch we were supposed to go see the grounds but it was still raining like crazy. The lights kept flickering so Jennifer and Vlad started lighting all the candles and they were weird looking."

"Why?"

"Man, they were really long and black with this red stripe down the middle. I touched one of them and Raquel freaked. She knocked it out of my hand and started saying all this stuff. That Vlad guy got this look on his face and made the sigh of the cross at her. It was like something out of an old movie like he was warding off the devil or something."

The Commander shook his head.

"That really ticked her off and she went after him. I grabbed her arm and she swung around and clawed my face."

"Is that how you got those scratches?"

"Yes."

"It was just about then that Jennifer or whatever her name was, that tour leader babe, came into the room and said we had to stay the night. Thanks to the rain something had happened to the road and there was no way to get down the mountain. We were each given a key to some old guest bedrooms on the second floor. Raquel grabbed ours and stormed off. I had to chase after her and she wouldn't say a word to me."

The Commander puffed on his pipe and contemplated the young American before him. He knew he wasn't lying and was confident the man wouldn't start now.

"I figured she was just mad and would get over it after a while. I chased her to the room and then she wouldn't let me in. She just slapped me in the face and then shut the door. I heard the lock go and I pounded on the door. Didn't do any good, so finally I wandered back downstairs. I was going to go see Jennifer and talk to her about getting a different room."

"Did you find her?"

"No, man. Maybe she was with Vlad."

He smirked and the Commander didn't react.

He wasn't sure what the whole story was on her just yet.

"Okay, so then what did you do?"

"I wandered around the castle, man. I didn't see anybody. I went into a bunch of different rooms. You ever been in there?"

"Everyone in the village has been inside at one time or another."

"Its weird, man. It's like a maze. You go down a hall and sometimes you think you have been there before and sometimes you don't. Rooms lead into rooms and it's like you are wandering some sort of maze."

Of course he was. *The castle has many secrets and does not surrender them willingly.*

"Then, Vlad suddenly shows up. One second he isn't there and then bang, he is there. He gestures to me and I follow him and suddenly we are back in the main hall. There is this long banquet table laid out and all this food. Raquel is there in this fantastic white gown that made her look really hot. Cut down in the front and back, the gown clung to her like it was her skin, man and all the guys were staring at her."

Lost in the moment, the suspect shifted in his chair. The Commander understood. Raquel had appeared to him once in much the same way in what seemed to have had been a lifetime ago. He knew well what the American had felt and knew that it had led unquestionably to one conclusion. He nodded to him and the suspect nodded back and looked down at the table.

"So, after we ate, we went back to the room. Raquel led me down the hallway and once we were back in the room, she lit all these candles. Then, she let the gown slip off her shoulders and we…."

"I understand. You don't have to explain. What happened after that?"

"I must have fallen asleep or something."

Something indeed.

"I woke up and the windows were open. I could hear wolves, coyotes, something like that howling. The candles were all out and I realized Raquel wasn't in the bed beside me. I had a really bad headache and it took me a minute or two to get my feet on the floor. I staggered across the room and looked out the window."

He stopped and the Commander puffed on his pipe waiting for him. From the far away look in the suspect's eyes, he was seeing it again.

"Raquel was out there and there were these things around her. Big black things. Not wolves but sort of like wolves and they were circling around her. I don't know what they were. It had stopped raining and the moon was out and it was like the moonlight was focused right on her. She was all lit up and then there were those things circling around her. I wanted to scream at her, to warn her, but I couldn't."

The Commander shook his head slowly.

"Man, I didn't know what was happening. Then one of those big black creature things looked up at me. Weird yellow eyes and it was like I heard something in my head. It was just one word. *Food.* Suddenly they all were looking up at me and so was Raquel. Then she made this gesture and they all vanished into the trees.

"I stood there at the window trying to see where she went. After a couple of minutes, I heard her scream. Then something howled and she screamed again. I looked but there was no way I could get out through the window so I grabbed my shoes and ran downstairs.

"I guess I must have put them on and all because the next thing I know I am running across the lawn towards those trees. It's all white and funny around me, almost like it is daytime and I look up and the moon is huge. I can see the winged things flying across the face of it and they are heading the same way. Somehow I know they are thinking about me and know I am no threat. I look back at the castle and there is this greenish light coming out from every window and shooting out the turrets at the top. I stop and stare for a moment and then something tells me to run."

He stopped and stared hard at the Commander.

"I know you think I'm nuts, but I saw things, man. Things you would not believe."

You would be surprised my young American friend if I could tell you. I can't. For the first time in along time, he felt a twinge of regret regarding a suspect's fate. Still, a deal was a deal. "Right now, it doesn't matter what I believe. I just need you to tell me what you saw."

The man nodded, swallowed and went on, his voice trembling with emotion. His dark eyes widened and his fingers on his right hand twitched spasmodically.

So did the twin hooks high above stirred by the raw emotional energy emanating from him.

He will do nicely for them, the Commander thought as he listened once more to the tale.

"Finally, I break out into this clearing. Raquel is standing in the middle of the clearing with her hands raised up to the sky. She is chanting something—I don't know what—with her hands fully extended above her. Those black things, more than a dozen of them, are circling around her and howling. The winged creatures are circling in the air above her, as well. Her voice goes way up, and she flails her hands at the sky and suddenly the air is filled with lightening.

"It was like some sort of movie, man. Bolts of lightening are hitting the ground all around her and the cliff tops, and she's standing there screaming at the sky. Her long white robe vanishes and she's naked and I couldn't help but get turned on. She had that way, you know? You just saw her and you got aroused. I mean here she is in this clearing above the castle with the crags of the mountains around her getting hit by bolts of lightening, weird black things circling around her and these other winged things in the air, and all I can think about is how hot she looks and how bad I want her. It was all real and powerful and then she goes and ruins it."

"What do you mean?"

"She floated off the ground, man. She lifted right up and started flying! That just doesn't happen. I mean you have to have suspension of disbelief to buy this stuff and then she goes and flies."

He sat back and stared at the Commander.

"Don't you get it? She floated! It just wasn't possible. I couldn't believe in her anymore. I knew it all had to be a dream. It wasn't real."

"It was all a dream? A mere figment of your imagination?"

"Had to be."

"How do you explain the blood in your room? How do you explain Raquel's body being found in the clearing covered in bite marks? The scratches on your face?"

"It didn't happen. It's all part of the same stupid dream. I'm still dreaming."

"You are awake."

"According to you. Would I dream it otherwise?"

"What else have you done in this long dream of yours?"

"I called home and told them I was having a wonderful time."

"You did?"

"I did. Can't have the parents worrying or they would decide I need rehab again."

"Even in your dreams?"

The suspect laughed but there was no humor in it.

"Especially there." The suspect sat back and yawned before adding, "I haven't lost my mind, Commander. I just can't wake up."

"You have told no one else."

He shook his head, exhausted from trying to explain it all.

"Written nothing down? Not even for your mother, the novelist?"

"She wouldn't care. She writes romances."

The Commander knew what she wrote but he had to be sure. She would be watched—her writings, both published and unpublished analyzed for any sign of the legacy. Ever since that damn thriller novel nonsense from a couple of years ago it was a lot harder to keep conspiracies secret.

"So, no one knows of what you saw or 'dreamed' as you put it?"

"Nope. Nobody."

Good.

"Okay, I need to see to some manners upstairs and I will be back in a few minutes. I want you to think about whether or not you saw anything else and want to tell me."

"It's all a dream, man."

The suspect sat back and grinned at the Commander who stood up and walked out of the room closing the door softly behind him. After all these years he still wasn't sure exactly what happened when he left the prisoners behind and really didn't want to know. He had done as he had been told and there was no record of the suspect telling anyone. He believed all of it to be a dream no doubt inspired by his anti-depression medication.

The young man, new to this command by two weeks was waiting outside of his office when the Commander arrived. He followed him inside and stood at attention in front of the desk.

"Yes?"

"I was wondering how it went with the suspect, Sir?"

"It went fine. It doesn't concern you at this point. You have other duties to attend to."

Normally, that was enough to get even the most politically unaware rookie out of his office. Instead, the young man stepped back exactly one step and sat down in the chair in front of the desk.

The Commander stared at him, his anger mounting until he saw the flash in the man's eyes. To others it would have been unnoticeable but for him, thanks to the deal he had made long ago, it was a neon sign as to the power across the desk from him.

"He knows nothing. He thinks it was all a dream." He gestured around the room with his free hand while his other tensed and readied to reach for the gun mounted underneath the lap drawer. All he had to do was touch it and it would fire a special round right through the desk and into anyone, or anything, unlucky enough to be sitting across from him. "He believes everything happening to be a dream."

"Good."

"My thoughts exactly."

"I'm sure they were. Now, what do we do about you?"

The Commander reached for the gun and found it missing. The holster was still there, mocking him in its emptiness and his chance was gone.

The young man snickered and suddenly held the gun pointed at the Commander's forehead.

"You were told to keep no records."

"I wrote nothing!"

"You wrote journals. You talked about your feelings. Being a male, you were chosen for this assignment because you weren't supposed to have feelings." The young man shrugged his shoulders and looked at him the same way the Commander had looked at many before they went on their final journey. "You should have known that writing a journal was a bad idea. It gives one strange thoughts. Thoughts have actions. Actions have consequences."

He fired one shot directly through the Commander's forehead. The bullet, designed to kill a non-human entity, pulverized the Commander's head, spraying long arcs of brain matter and blood across the widows behind him. Windows blazed with the sun as it came above the horizon signaling the start of another Easter Sunday.

"Suicide on Easter Sunday. How sad."

The young man chuckled as he walked out of the room his first assignment complete. Being related to Lord John Erdely had its privileges and he had a date with a certain tour guide operator.

AUTHOR'S BIO: In addition to having been the editor or assistant editor of several different zines, my book reviews appear extensively online and I am the book reviewer for the Texas edition of the newspaper "Senior News." My short fiction has appeared in magazines such as "Lynx Eye," "Starblade," "Show and Tell," and "The Writer's Post Journal" among others and online at such places as "Mouth Full Of Bullets," "Crime And Suspense," "Mysterical-e" and others.

Thicker than Stone
By
Christina Barber

"Hurry up, Harry, or we'll miss the bus!" Meredyth Bancroft yelled at her husband. With one hand on the doorknob and the other placed firmly upon her hip, she tapped her foot.

Harry puttered along. He was always late. Even on vacation.

"Just one more minute, I've got to get the camera." Harry went about his business, ignoring his wife's sighs. Nothing fazed Harry.

"Let's go," Harry said, finally, smiling as if he hadn't been the reason for the delay.

Meredyth closed the door and raced down the hall of the Hotel Cornifu. Harry trudged behind. As they entered the elevator Harry started to say something, then paused. Instead, he slipped his hand into hers and grinned.

Meredyth looked at Harry then at her watch. She released Harry's hand.

"Oh, I hope we didn't miss the bus, Harry. I really do want to see Lord Erdely's Castle."

The elevator buzzed and when the doors opened, Meredyth took off running, like a horse at the Kentucky Derby. Harry exited slowly. He had no desire to head off to yet another castle.

They'd spent the last two weeks traipsing across the Carpathian Mountains of Austria, Hungary, Poland and now Rumania. Harry was getting tired of sightseeing, especially when he thought all the sites looked alike. But, he'd promised Meredyth they would go see this one last castle, especially since this tour's price tag suited his style—it was free.

Rounding the corner of the front door to the hotel, Harry saw Meredyth climbing up the steps of a shiny tourist bus. Reluctantly, he joined her and the doors squeaked as they slammed shut behind him. Rain pelted the windshield and the wipers worked at full speed, though they barely cleared all of the oncoming water. The driver eased the bus into gear.

Harry chose the first available seat and they sat on the hot, crowded bus. He leaned over and whispered into Meredyth's ear, "Are you sure this is the right tour?"

Meredyth removed a letter from her purse and waved over the young brunette seated at the front.

"Welcome aboard."

Meredyth thrust the letter at the young lady. "Are we on the right bus? I got this special invitation."

"Well, let's see." The young lady scanned the letter and handed it back to Meredyth. "Yep, you are at the right place, Harry and Meredyth. I'm Jennifer, your tour guide. I'm glad you made it."

The bus shook and bounced from the bumpy road and Jennifer grabbed onto the seatback in front of her to steady her balance. She made her way to the front again and picked up a microphone.

"I'd like to welcome you all once again. We're in for a bit of a ride tonight, but sit back and enjoy the scenery. Oh, and if you have any questions about the castle, I'll be happy to answer them."

Meredyth spoke up. "So, it says here in my invitation that the castle is haunted. Does that mean it's going to be like that ride at Disney—remember that one, Harry?" She poked at his leg, "because, we don't like kiddy rides and we also don't frighten easily, especially when they use those cheap special effects."

Harry slumped in the seat. He remembered their trip to Disney well. That was when the kids were still small. The boys were now teens. Even back then, Meredyth could embarrass him.

Jennifer laughed. "No, it will be more of like . . . well, an investigation. We'll be able to walk around the castle, and judge for ourselves. I have some professional tools we will use, cameras, digital voice recorders, thermal scanner, motion detectors, and electromagnetic field detectors. I'll teach you how to use them and we'll conduct our own research."

Meredyth spoke to Harry through half-closed lips, "If she thinks I'm going to run around and play *Ghost Busters*, she's nuts."

Harry nodded and rolled his eyes. He pictured those guys on TV, running around in the dark, snapping pictures and trying to scare the viewers into thinking something evil lurked around the corner. It was all a bunch of malarkey.

Meredyth struck a conversation with the lady seated across from her. They compared notes about the dusty, old castles they'd each been visiting. Harry settled into the seat and closed his eyes. His head occasionally bounced on the window, but the soothing patter of the rain on the metal roof of the bus lulled him to sleep.

* * * *

Harry walked down the grey, stone, spiral staircase. He felt at ease, a certain, strange comfort of belonging to this place. At the bottom of the staircase he turned left and entered the large dining room flanked by suits of armor. A slight breeze came from the other end of the room, disturbing the tapestry on the wall. Footsteps echoed in the long hallway.

Instinctively, he pressed his back against the wall, attempting to hide from the intruder. He felt his skin mutate and harden. Harry watched as the wall sucked him in, consuming him completely.

****

Harry woke gasping for air.

"Lord, Harry. What's wrong with you?" Meredyth shook her head. "You were snoring again, and it's embarrassing."

Harry felt as if everyone on the bus stared at him, their judgmental eyes burning a whole in his chest.

"Sorry." Harry grinned sheepishly.

Conversations resumed after a few moments, and Harry closed his eyes again. This time however, he felt too unnerved from the bizarre dream to sleep.

The bus drove up a hill and they could see a large castle, looming in the distance. Again, Jennifer stood up and spoke into the microphone.

"We're just about there. We'll pull the bus as close to the entrance as possible, but I'm afraid we'll get a bit wet. I haven't seen weather like this in years. We'll get you all safely inside then get settled in."

The wind shook the bus and the rain bombarded the windows just as she made her statement.

"Yeah, I bet. Weather like this is better to scare the tourists. Huh, Harry?" Meredyth said sarcastically.

"Yes, dear. You're right."

The bus inched its way up the hill. With the castle in view the bus stopped. The driver sign-languaged to Jennifer. She nodded then shook her head.

Jennifer picked up the microphone. "Well, I have some bad news here, folks."

Everyone's attention focused on Jennifer. "It seems we're stuck. We can't get any closer, nor can we turn back. We'll have to walk the rest of the way."

A few tourists groaned.

The bus driver once again signaled something to Jennifer. She nodded.

"Um, well, there's more," she paused and blushed, then continued, "Vlad said we're going to have to stay here until the weather clears, he can't move the bus—we're stuck deep in the mud and if he tries to go anywhere we could end up in a mudslide."

Murmurs arose from the tourists. A sense of panic washed over the crowd like ocean waves.

"We'll get off the bus in an orderly fashion. Please make sure you take all of your belongings. First rows please follow me."

Meredyth winked at Harry.

He knew what she was thinking. Meredyth believed this was all part of the scare, a game or show, and she just played along. Harry felt differently, but he didn't say anything to his wife. They all followed Jennifer.

Even though the air felt warm, the breeze and the cold rain penetrated the skin and caused Meredyth to shiver. Harry took his jacket off and placed it over her shoulders.

He looked up at the enormous structure. Complete with turrets it looked like something out of a horror story. Each of the towers had a gargoyle statue perched at the very edge, like they were guarding the castle.

Everyone was soaked by the time they stepped inside the castle. Their clothes dripped on the stone floor creating individual puddles at their feet.

Harry put his arms around Meredyth trying to keep her warm. He thought about the reason, the whole purpose for the trip to Europe, to reconnect with Meredyth. He loved his wife dearly, but mid-life combined with stress reduced the couple to a roommate marriage.

Meredyth pushed Harry's arms off her shoulders and strode up to Jennifer.

"If we're stuck here, then there must be some kind of sleeping arrangements, right?"

"Well, I guess . . . we will need to figure all that out right now . . . so we can get settled in." Jennifer shook the remaining water from her clothes.

She walked to the table in the large entranceway and picked up a flashlight. "Grab a flashlight and follow me."

The entire group followed. Everyone shone their lights in different directions, casting an eerie shadow play upon the walls.

Again, Meredyth quietly spoke to Harry. "Oops, no power." She grinned, an evil, all knowing smile.

They all crept silently up the grey stone stairs as if not to disturb someone sleeping in the chambers. The distant howl of a wolf echoed into the immense castle and stopped them in their tracks. Jennifer motioned to continue the ascent. On the landing of the staircase on the second floor, the group awaited further instructions from Jennifer.

"We have enough rooms for each couple in the group. The layout for the castle is such that these rooms are all in one hallway," she motioned with her hand, "here."

Everyone stood expectantly, waiting for her to continue.

"So, go ahead and just grab a room. You can put your belongings in there. We should be quite comfortable here. Get settled in and meet me in the main entranceway in about ten minutes."

Couples broke off from the large group. Each picked a room. Meredyth and Harry selected the room at the end of the hall, one furthest from the staircase and entranceway.

Once they were inside the room and the door shut, Meredyth said, "Well, let's see. We have to stay here tonight, the weather is terrible, and there's a wolf outside the castle." She feigned a shriek. "Eek", then laughed.

Harry spoke softly, "Meredyth, darling, I really don't think this was supposed to happen. Look at it this way, would they let us stay here for free?"

Meredyth looked thoughtful. "Harry, you are so gullible. I'm sure they have a deal with the hotel so it's all included—you know, like those all-inclusive resorts."

She kissed his partially bald head and grinned. "Let's go see what other scares they have in store for us."

Harry grimaced, yet followed his wife out the bedroom door.

As Harry walked down the hall he felt as if someone watched his every move. He shivered and looked around nervously. When they descended the long staircase and entered the main hall, a bright flash of lightening struck, illuminating the dark entranceway. A few of the ladies screamed.

Jennifer calmed the gathering.

"It's just a bad storm, folks. As far as the ghosts—If there are any here, they won't harm you. So honestly, there's nothing to be afraid of. What we'll do is organize ourselves into teams of . . . "

While Jennifer gave instructions for the hunt, Harry stared past her. The long, dark hallway was foreboding, but there was something oddly familiar about the castle. He closed his eyes and pictured the layout of the building. Somehow he knew the exact design of the castle.

"Let's go, Harry." Meredyth handed Harry a voice recorder.

She placed the camera strap around her neck and walked down the hall.

"Wait," Harry said quietly.

She turned and faced Harry, a look of an agitated "What!" on her face.

"That's the wrong way. Let's go this way," Harry said, walking toward the staircase.

"Harry, I don't want to go back upstairs. I want to go wander the castle, look around a bit."

Harry walked to the area underneath the staircase and pressed a small inset stone.

A door opened revealing a set of spiral, stone stairs.

Meredyth looked on with amazement. "How did you...?"

Harry shrugged and walked through the door.

Meredyth followed.

Using the flashlights, they made their way down the long set of stairs. A musty scent of decay accosted their senses when they made it to the bottom.

"Ugh, what is that horrible smell?" Meredyth croaked as she held her nose.

Harry couldn't focus on the smell. A bizarre feeling washed over him, from his feet to the tip of his nose, and back again. It felt as if his skin tightened then cracked.

Meredyth moved her flashlight beam onto Harry. Her eyes grew large with fear and her mouth hung open. Then she let out a blood-curdling scream.

Harry moved his flashlight to focus on his arm. He expected to see a large, hairy spider. Instead, he watched as his skin rippled with mottled grays that looked like marble—the same stone of the castle.

Harry heard footsteps approaching, clamoring down the steps. Terrified by his own appearance, he darted into the pitch-black room. There, he ran into the corner and sat in a chair. Oddly enough he could see fairly well in the room, and didn't trip over any furniture. He sat panting.

Meredyth called out. "Harry! Where are you?" Her voice shook with fear. She didn't move from the stairwell.

Other people arrived. Jennifer accompanied the small group. "What's wrong, Meredyth? What happened?"

"It's Harry, something's wrong with him. His skin was all weird and now he's missing!"

"Missing?"

"Yes. He ran that way." Meredyth pointed toward the room.

"There is safety in numbers, so let's go in that direction and see if we can find him, okay?"

Jennifer led the group from the stairs into the room. The light from their flashlights swirled all around. Bookshelves covered every wall and upon the shelves sat thousands of tomes. Cobwebs covered much of the furniture and a thick layer of dust lay upon the stone floor. The room felt cold and forbidding.

Harry buried his face in his hands and curled up on the chair, in hopes no one would see him.

"Harry?" Jennifer said, focusing her light on him.

Harry looked at the group through slightly opened fingers—normal colored fingers.

Slowly, he moved his hand away paying careful attention to his skin. Everything appeared normal and he felt like himself again.

Meredyth raced over to Harry, throwing her arms around him. "Oh, Harry, I'm so glad you're okay!"

Harry stood, speechless.

Jennifer came over to Harry and Meredyth. "Perhaps you two should take it easy. Why don't you go up and rest a bit?"

Meredyth shot Jennifer an angry look. "No thank you. We want to keep looking around. Right, Harry?"

Jennifer frowned. "Do you both feel you're up to this?"

"Yes. I feel just fine. Perhaps it was all the excitement that got us thinking we'd seen something," Harry said, as he stood.

"Very well, then. Carry on everyone. Oh, Meredyth and Harry, I didn't know this room existed. How did you find it?"

Meredyth looked at Harry who scratched his balding head and shrugged. After a few moments of silence he stammered his answer. "I . . . well, something led me here. I actually can't really explain. I guess you can call it dumb luck."

Jennifer laughed. "Well, I call it wonderful. We've heard rumors of this – this room we're in—being the dungeon. However, none of our other groups were successful in finding the hidden lever."

Harry swallowed hard before he spoke. "Um, Jennifer, are there other rumors about the castle or of Lord Erdely?"

The crowd intensely focused on Jennifer.

"Well, there's not much we know about Lord Erdely. Some information tells he constantly fought with the Orthodox Church. Many people speculated he practiced black magic, but there's no proof. Rumors said he would blind and deafen his servants when they traveled into town – apparently to keep his secrets safe."

A young woman spoke. "So, who do you think these ghosts are who haunt the castle?"

Jennifer shook her head. "Well, since we can't exactly ask them, we can only guess. We think it's probably some of the servants."

"Not Lord Erdely, too?" Another person asked.

"No. We don't believe so. Can't really explain why, but we just don't get the feeling it's him."

Everyone hung on Jennifer's words. A few people shifted their weight nervously or rubbed their hands upon their arms—keeping the cold and goose bumps away.

"Well, enough on what we don't know. Let's go see if we can find some proof," Jennifer said, in a light, happy tone.

After a few minutes, several people went upstairs. Jennifer soon followed. Harry and Meredyth lingered after the others left.

Once the footsteps ceased their beat upon the stairs, Meredyth spoke. "Harry, I know what I saw. Granted it was very odd, but I know you looked. . ."

"Like stone," Harry said, finishing her statement.

"Yes. Like stone." Meredyth walked over to the stairway landing and waved her arms around. "Maybe we tripped some kind of special effect when we came down here."

Harry slowly walked over to her. He stood on the last step. "Meredyth, honey, I felt strange. It felt like my skin was cracking."

"Harry, that's because of the heat from whatever effect they used."

Harry knew better than to argue. He nodded and walked up the stairs; Meredyth followed.

After walking around the castle until eleven at night, the entire group reconvened in the main hall. Jennifer stood in the middle of the large hall and gathered all the equipment.

"In the morning, we'll have the kitchen up and running. Sleep well, and for any reason, you need anything, I'll be in the first room."

Many goodnights were exchanged as everyone walked upstairs and went to bed.

Harry reluctantly crawled into bed. He didn't want to sleep, he felt too nervous. He lay next to Meredyth as she peacefully slumbered. She never had difficulty sleeping—anywhere. Harry closed his eyes and a few minutes later, fell fast asleep.

* * * *

Harry stood in the main entranceway. Servants bustled about the castle. He watched the scene briefly before moving down the long hallway. He felt light, almost like floating across the room. He soared above the ground, climbing higher into the air with every passing minute. Over his shoulder, large gray wings flapped as he flew across the castle. His skin, was, once again, a marbleized gray.

No one looked up nor saw him. He seemed to blend into the coloration of the building. Harry felt a sense of duty – to protect the castle and all who entered it. He flew out an open window and to the top of the castle. Perched high upon a turret, gripping it tightly with his talons…

* * * *

Harry's eyes flew open. It took a few moments to familiarize himself with his surroundings. He looked at his skin and felt a sense of relief, yet also disappointment, when he saw the pinkish, yellow tones of normal, human skin.

Harry stood and walked over to the enormous window in the bedroom peering out into the moonless night. Droplets of rain trickled down the panes. A gust of wind blew the boughs of a tree, scraping them against the window.

Again, Harry felt as if he belonged here—to this castle. He felt a calling, a purpose unlike any other before.

Leaning onto the windowsill, he peered up at the turret over their window. A gargoyle sat looking at Harry, blinking its ruby eyes. Harry jumped back in terror, but felt pangs of curiosity. He ran to the bedside and shook Meredyth awake. "Merry, wake up, honey, please!"

"Huh, Harry?" she said sleepily.

"Come here. I need to show you something." He tugged on her hand like a child.

"Okay, okay." She trundled out of bed.

Harry ran to the window. "Look—there's a gargoyle. And it's alive!"

Meredyth rubbed her eyes, yawned, and looked out the window in the direction of the gargoyle.

Harry stood grinning.

Meredyth shook her head. "Yeah, it's a gargoyle, but that thing is made of stone. It's certainly not alive, Harry."

She started to move away but Harry pushed her toward the window.

"Wait! Look again! I'm telling 'ya, that thing blinked at me."

Meredyth moved around Harry and toward the bed. "I'm going back to sleep. I suggest you do the same."

Harry looked out the window again. The gargoyle sat perched on the edge of the ledge with its back to Harry.

There was no explanation to what he witnessed, but he knew what he'd seen—the gargoyle was alive.

Unable to sleep, Harry sat on the chair in the corner of the room. He positioned himself so he could see out the window and watch the gargoyle.

After a few minutes the stone figure moved. It turned around and faced Harry. Again it blinked.

Harry sat motionless, watching the creature. It shuffled about on the turret, stretched its wings, and repositioned itself on the edge of the wall.

Harry's curiosity piqued, he couldn't contain himself any longer. He darted out of the bedroom, down the castle stairs and out the front door. He moved around the side of the enormous structure. The rain pelted his skin and drenched his clothes as he ran through the woods. When he reached the bottom of the turret, he looked up at the looming figure.

"I saw you move," he shouted. "I know you're real."

The gargoyle didn't move.

"I know what you are," Harry yelled again. "I'm one of you!"

After the words left his lips, he wished he'd never spoken them. The gargoyle swooped down, landing inches away from Harry. Although it looked like it was made of stone, it moved fluidly.

Its voice sounded harsh and thick, almost grumbled. It was not English, but Harry understood.

"Are you?"

Harry couldn't move and shivered with fear.

The gargoyle hopped along the ground surveying every inch of Harry. Then it stood in front of him again. "Yes, yes! Son of H. T Bancroft!" the gargoyle exclaimed in his language. "You stay. Do job."

"Job? I don't work here. I don't even live here, I'm on vacation."

The gargoyle shook his head. "So, must choose!"

Harry felt faint. He was confused and scared.

The gargoyle jumped along the ground briefly then ascended to the turret once again.

It all seemed surreal. Harry felt dizzy and the world tilted; he stumbled then fell into the leaves and blacked out.

* * * *

Harry woke shivering and soaked. He realized he'd spent some of the night outside, passed out in the leaves. The sun had begun to crest over the horizon. The rain had stopped.

Briefly confused, Harry looked around. When he saw the gargoyle on the wall, his memory returned. He remembered the gargoyle saying something about a choice and a job. *What choice?* Harry wondered.

He walked inside and to the kitchen. Jennifer busied preparing breakfast for the guests. She jumped as Harry walked in.

"I didn't think anyone else was awake yet. You gave me a fright."

Harry sat down on a stool. Jennifer pulled out a coffee mug.

"Want some coffee?"

"Yes, please."

"Um, Jennifer. Do you know anything about the gargoyles here at the castle?"

Jennifer thought briefly, before answering. "No, can't say that I do. I know in legends they are the protectors of the castle and the Lord. Why?"

He scrambled for an answer. "Oh, I was admiring them last night. Thought they were special."

Jennifer handed Harry a cup of coffee.

"Yeah, they are kinda neat, aren't they?" Jennifer flipped the bacon in the pan. "So, did you see any evidence of ghosts last night?"

"No, don't think we did."

Jennifer shook her head and sighed. "I didn't either."

Other guests arrived in the kitchen and soon the smell of eggs and bacon filled the air.

Everyone dug into the amazing smelling food, except Harry. He didn't have much of an appetite. Meredyth arrived and shoveled scrambled eggs onto her plate. She sat next to Harry.

"Well, since everyone is here," Jennifer said, "let's discuss our findings from last night."

A few said they'd seen a ghostly figure wandering the halls. Everyone sat in utter amazement as they described a shadowy being and an orb of shooting light.

Jennifer explained about orbs and how they are energy.

"So, after we pack, we can leave. Let's shoot for two o'clock today and meet in the foyer."

Everyone felt relieved to know they were going back to the hotel, everyone, except Harry.

Harry went exploring later that morning. He wanted to go back downstairs to the library and see if there was anything on gargoyles in the extensive collection of books.

Grabbing a flashlight he opened the secret door. Again, he surprised himself with the ease it took to find it—a knowing.

He crept slowly down the stairs and into the dark, musty room. Scanning the spines of the books on each shelf, he saw many interesting titles, especially ones on black magic. One nearly jumped off the shelf. Harry grabbed the book titled, *Family History*, and plopped into the chair. He read all the names of servants and workers employed by Lord Erdely, every bit of it handwritten, presumably by Lord Erdely himself.

Harry stopped, his eyes widened when he found the page titled *Gargoyles*. An entire list of names filled the page. And at the very bottom he saw it, Harry Theodore Bancroft – his great-great grandfather and his namesake.

Harry had been told stories of his great-great grandfather. About how he went to work for a Lord in some castle and the family never heard from him again. Harry always thought his family made it up, to scare the grandchildren.

It seemed so odd, almost crazy. Harry was a direct descendant of a gargoyle, his great-something grandfather. For once in his life, he felt like he belonged.

However, it sounded strange, even to Harry, when he tried to explain it to Meredyth in the room later that day.

"Meredyth, I really don't know how to explain it to you, but there's something very special about this place."

She laughed. "Yeah, it's old and dusty. Special all right. Now I know why the tour was free."

Harry tried again. "No! This castle is magical."

"Harry, it's your imagination running off with you. Just like last night and that statue."

Harry felt humiliated. In anger and shame, he walked over to the wall and wished he'd disappear – just like in his dream—be invisible yet there.

He felt an odd sensation, his skin ached, then started turning into that gray marbleized color. The same way it had last night. Bones popped out of his back. His shirt ripped and his clothes fell to the ground.

Meredyth spent the time applying make-up and never saw her husband transform.

Harry stood still, silent, against the stone wall. Finally, Meredyth turned and looked at the pile of clothes on the floor.

"Ugh, Harry, what are you doing?" She looked around the room.

She opened the bedroom door and peered into the hallway. She closed the door and spoke again, "Harry, are you playing some kind of sick game?" She looked under the bed and around the room. Even right at Harry.

She grabbed his clothes and stormed out of the bedroom. Harry followed. He slinked across the wall without difficulty and watched as she went down and met the group in the main hallway.

"I can't find my husband."

Jennifer looked perplexed. "Okay, well, I guess we can all do a search."

Jennifer assembled teams of four and everyone set out.

"Harry!" His name was called over and over.

He didn't move, not even a flinch. He just stayed melded, and one with the wall, as a gargoyle.

Hours later, when the sun began to set, the group boarded the bus. Jennifer consoled Meredyth as she sobbed into Harry's clothes.

Harry moved out the door and up to the turret. A wolf howled in the distance.

Jennifer held Meredyth's hand. "Mrs. Bancroft, I'm so sorry. We'll send a search party when we get into town. I'm afraid we are the only ones up here and with the darkness setting it, we really need to get going."

Meredyth wailed then stepped onto the bus.

Jennifer spoke to another guest, "If he isn't inside the castle, I'm afraid they won't find him alive. The terrain is too unforgiving."

The man nodded.

They climbed aboard and the bus slowly climbed to the top of the hill. The driver turned the bus and started down the hill.

Harry watched from his perch on the castle turret. He felt pangs of sorrow for the loss of his children. But he was meant to stay here, in a very special place, performing a very unique job—a gargoyle guard for Lord Erdely, just as his great-great grandfather had done many, many years before.

He watched as the bus disappeared down the hill, around the bend and out of his sight. In one swift motion he leapt up, spread his great stone-like wings and ascended to his rightful place on the castle wall.

AUTHOR'S BIO: Christina Barber is an award-winning author of speculative fiction works noted for their dark tones. When Christina's not scanning dusty old books for interesting tidbits of mythology, she's off writing in her dark fantasy worlds.

Encouraged by her fourth grade teacher, Christina has always been captivated by the craft of writing, and recently made the move to full-time writer.

Christina's published books include Seely's Pond (Dark Urban Fantasy, March 2008), Ghosts of Southern Crescent, Georgia (Non-Fiction, Summer 2008) and Greystone (2006 Speculative Romance). She has short stories appearing in magazines and anthologies across the writing spectrum.

While Christina spent most of her life growing up in the suburbs of New Jersey, she currently resides in Newnan, Georgia with her husband and daughter. She happily shares her home with three dogs, and two cats.

To learn more about Christina, visit her website at www.christinabarber.net

THE SCHOLAR
By
Seana Graham

"Hello? Is anybody there?"

Howard Green pounded yet again on the heavy wooden door, more aware now of its sturdiness than of the traditional Transylvanian pattern he'd been so charmed by when he'd walked up to it five minutes ago. Reluctantly, he faced the prospect that the handwritten sign taped to the door might apply to him as much as the rest of the general public. You didn't have to be an expert in Eastern European antiquities—although, in fact, he was—to understand that "ÎNCHIS" was Romanian for "CLOSED."

"*Scuză-mă!*" he called out to a passing workman, who stopped and stared at him noncommittally. "Art. Hot. *Bibliotecă.*" Howard stopped. He could read medieval texts well enough if he had a dictionary close to hand, but that didn't mean he was fluent in modern-day Romanian. "Do you speak English?"

The workman shrugged.

"The li-brar-y," he said, as though he were speaking to someone who was hard of hearing. "When will it open?"

The man walked up to the sign and looked at it. He turned to Howard. "*Închis,*" he said. "Is close-ed."

"I know it's closed," Howard said in exasperation. "I'm asking when it will be open. *Deschidere. Capisci?*" The first word Romanian, the second not, but Howard had a tendency to view the romance languages as largely interchangeable.

The man stared at the sign again for a long time, though what further enlightenment he could glean from it, Howard could not see. "Is not soon," he said.

"Not soon? So, what, a few hours?"

"No, no—sorry, sir, no."

"Tomorrow?" The man shook his head. "But I'm only here for the week. I've planned my whole trip around seeing the collection here at the college!"

"Is close-ed this month."

"That's impossible!"

The workman said nothing, only looked expressively at the sign. He brightened suddenly. "Repair-ations!" he said triumphantly. "Is close-ed for repair-ations."

"Reparations?" He thought about it. "Repairs? You mean repairs? But why wasn't I informed?" Howard asked, though he could hardly have expected the man to know the answer.

It didn't matter. The workman was already moving on.

* * * *

By the next evening, Howard was ready to write off Cornifu and its blasted library entirely and move on to the next town on his itinerary, though the rare texts on the relics, ruins and pagan practices of the Carpathian Mountains rumored to lie behind that locked door would very likely tantalize him forever. But a day spent looking for the librarian, or even anyone with a key to the place had proved to be in vain. It was now time to head back to the hotel and dress for dinner.

He and his wife, Elizabeth, were joining his Romanian colleague, Stefan Petrescu, while they were here. He'd first met Stefan back at Radley College, where Petrescu had been a visiting professor for a year. Howard and Elizabeth had both taken a shine to the charming academic, and often had him over during his sojourn there. Tonight, he was reciprocating by taking them out to a nice restaurant not too far from their hotel. But even this was not an unalloyed pleasure. Petrescu had first whetted Howard's appetite about the library, and Howard was still a little miffed that Stefan hadn't bothered to notify him about the library's closure. The man had been apologetic, of course, but what good did an apology do Howard?

Elizabeth had begged off joining him on his hunt for the key, claiming a headache and saying she'd like to rest before their evening out. Howard suspected what she really wanted to do was escape from his black mood, which had hovered around him like a dark force field ever since his disappointing discovery about the library.

He got the key at the desk and walked up the two flights to the hotel room. Elizabeth was in the shower, her evening dress laid out on the bed. His own suit and tie were laid out as well, which mollified him a bit since it showed she'd at least been thinking of him.

He began to unbutton his shirt when he noticed the envelope lying on the dresser. Who'd be writing them here? No one but Stefan even knew they were in Cornifu, and it made no sense that he'd have taken the time to write them on this fancy stationary when he could reach them by telephone.

"Dear Doctor and Mrs. Howard Green:

We cordially invite you..."

Howard scanned it and then tossed it on the bed with a scoff. The thing had 'tourist scam' written all over it. He again felt the disappointment he'd been wrestling with all day. For a moment, it actually looked like something important, some official invitation. Whoever had sent it had clearly spent some money on the stationary, and that seal looked impressive enough. But it was obviously all built on the *pay a little upfront to make a lot more down the road* premise. Well, it would take more than fancy paper to reel him in, that was for sure.

President of the American Paranormal Association of World Tours, my eye.

He supposed that in a dump like Cornifu, you had to think up some way to get the tourists' dollars off them. They just weren't going to be Howard's dollars.

Elizabeth came out of the bathroom, toweling down her hair. *She looks younger*, Howard thought. It wasn't the first time he'd noticed it during the trip. Being in Transylvania seemed to be having a salutary effect on her health. *Must be all this mountain air*, he thought. *Or maybe it's just being away from home that does it.* After all, unlike him, *she* was actually on vacation. *Must be nice*, he thought begrudgingly, conveniently forgetting that it was *his* project that had been the original catalyst for this trip.

"Did you see the invitation?" Elizabeth asked, her eyes glowing with pleasure.

She's actually excited about this, Howard realized. He struggled to suppress his irritation.

"Surely you haven't fallen for this claptrap?"

She gave him an injured look. Obviously she had.

Howard sighed. Sometimes he felt he'd married the wrong woman.

"I don't see where the harm is," she ventured, hesitantly.

"Oh, I suppose there's no harm, if you don't count utterly wasting your time—and mine."

"Well, what else were you going to do tomorrow, now that the library is closed?"

The mention of the library aggrieved him afresh. "What do you mean, what am I going to do? I have a whole briefcase full of notes I've accumulated on this trip, in case you hadn't noticed."

"But couldn't we just stay here in Cornifu, as we'd planned? It's such a lovely little town, and Stefan has offered to show us the area."

"What is he going to show us—yet more of the peasant holdings? I think I've seen enough of them from the road, thank you."

"I'm sure he's found something to entertain us."

"Entertain you, maybe. He's a professor of literature. I'm sure he can make even this bucolic setting seem romantic. But I'm a textual scholar. I need primary sources. I have no time for fairy tales. I need something more solid to hold my interest."

"Well, a castle is surely solid enough, isn't it?"

"This has 'fake' written all over it, Elizabeth. Even you must be able to see that!"

"It's a real castle, Howard. There's a photograph of it in the lobby."

"Oh, I don't doubt that it's a real building. It may even have some historical significance for all I know, though I've never heard of any Lord Erdely, and you'd think I would have run across the name at some point in my studies. But I can guarantee you that any group calling itself the 'American Paranormal Association' isn't interested in history. They're just interested in putting a few chills up your spine and raking in some cash at the end of the day."

"But it's a free tour. It says so right on the invitation."

"And I'm sure they pass the hat round at some point and make everyone feel like a tightwad if they don't shell out."

"Well, I think a day trip to the castle sounds lovely. Maybe we can even persuade Stefan to join us up there for a picnic or something."

"If you want to go, I suppose I can't prevent you, though I think what these people are doing is a travesty of respectable research. No doubt they'll have some local yokel dressed up to look like Dracula popping out of a box at just the right time, and scare everyone silly. And then they'll all have a good laugh and go home. Never mind that there is true and ancient history in these parts. Never mind that the real scholars are always underfunded. Anyway, I'm not going. Ask Stefan to take my place if you want."

"But the invitation is specifically addressed to you."

"Have you been listening to a word I've been saying, Elizabeth? All these people want is another investor in whatever little scheme they've got going. Probably some timeshare would be my guess. Believe me—they aren't going to be asking anyone for I.D. when it comes to writing out the checks."

He caught her shooting him a disapproving glance. It was what Howard privately referred to as her *stubborn look*. It was as though she'd slipped a mask over her face, making her expression unreadable, but if he looked closely at her eyes he saw other things—mutiny quite possibly, disdain almost certainly. But he wanted the subject closed, and as usual, she at least gave the appearance of deferring to his wishes.

Experience had taught him, though, that this didn't necessarily mean she'd given in. If the past was any indicator, she was probably just biding her time before she made another sally. Still, he would have to put his foot down on this one. There was absolutely no way in hell she was getting him to go up to Lord Erdely's blasted castle.

* * * *

Stefan was waiting for them at the restaurant when they arrived, and stood to greet them as they were ushered to the table.

Now here's a man who could play Dracula, Howard thought as they approached. He had just the pale skin and dark eyes and shock of black hair, now graying in a rather distinguished way at the temples, to do it. Howard had the height on him, but somehow Stefan's smaller frame always made Howard feel like a big bumbling oaf.

Elizabeth lit up when she saw him, of course. Howard had never felt particularly worried by Elizabeth's obvious attraction to Stefan. Stefan was quite the ladies' man. At least that was the rumor circulating during his year at Radley College. But Howard suspected his taste ran more to undergraduates and sexy young untenured teachers than to Howard's meek and rather mousy little wife, though he had to admit she didn't look so mousy tonight. There was no doubt about it—something in this place agreed with her.

"So there's really no way that I can get any access to the library?" Howard asked abruptly as soon as they were seated.

"Howard!" Elizabeth said, mortified. "Give us a chance to catch up with Stefan before you start badgering him, for heaven's sake."

"But it's the whole reason that we're here."

"It's not the whole reason that *I'm* here," Elizabeth said. "I'm sorry, Stefan. Howard can be very crass at times."

"No, don't apologize. He has the—how do you say?—bee in his bonnet about this library. I quite understand. I am the one to apologize for not knowing in advance. And, no, Howard, I am sorry to say that it is quite impossible to get in and see anything. The books are all stored away under plastic sheeting protecting them from the dust."

"Crap," Howard said.

"It will just be a good excuse to have you both back again one day," Stephan said. "What can't be helped, eh?" he shrugged. "Now, what shall we all do with this delightful weather we are having tomorrow?"

"Well, actually—" Elizabeth began.

Howard groaned.

Despite this, Elizabeth proceeded to tell Stefan about the invitation. "So as Howard isn't remotely interested in going," she concluded, "I was wondering if you might care to go with me in his place."

"Ah," Stefan said. "You see, this is a bit delicate."

"Hah! Look there, Lizzy. He has no more interest in going than I do. Have you ever been up there, Stefan?"

"Oh, yes—as a boy, plenty of times. As you say, it is rumored to be haunted, and my friends and I dared ourselves to a number of challenges up there. But this was long before this American group took over. I have no idea what it's like now."

"Aren't you curious, Stefan?" She sounded disappointed.

"I'm sorry, Elizabeth, I have not made myself clear. My reluctance has nothing to do with a lack of curiosity. It is Howard I am thinking of."

"Me? Why?"

"Well, it seems to me that it might not be prudent to refuse this invitation."

"I'm supposed to be afraid of offending this paranormal tour group?" Howard scoffed.

"No, not them."

"Well, who then?"

For the first time that evening, Petrescu looked uncomfortable. He ran his finger under his collar and then smiled nervously. "The walls have ears," he said quietly.

"I thought the Communist era was over," Howard said, loudly.

Elizabeth glared at him.

"The Communists were never the only ones with ears in Cornifu," Stefan said.

"Take a hint, Howard," Elizabeth said, quietly. She glanced at Stefan sympathetically.

"I'm sorry that you both find me so obtuse," Howard said, "but I really don't understand this. It was an invitation, not an order."

"Sometimes the two are not as different as you might suppose," Stefan said. He looked at Howard searchingly and then more kindly. "If I can put it this way—there are people in high places who might take offense at your lack of interest in Lord Erdely's castle."

"So?"

"So, you might find the rest of your journey through the Carpathians, shall we say, 'problematic'."

"Problematic? In what sense problematic? You're not suggesting that we'd be in any danger, are you?"

"Probably not," Petrescu said, although there was something in his tone that wasn't all that reassuring. "It's more a question of, how shall I put it? Of paperwork."

"Paperwork?"

"Permissions granted—or not. Entrance to certain historic sites expedited—or the reverse." He looked closely at Howard. "You have already seen how certain public buildings can be closed for repairs at a moment's notice. I think you could count on there being more such closures along your route."

"Are you saying that the library was closed on purpose?"

"I am not saying any such thing. It's more what I am not saying that you should be listening to, if you understand me."

Howard thought about this for a while. "And all I have to do is go on this blasted day trip for the, well, for the gods to be appeased, so to speak?"

"I think that would be the right course of action," Stefan said seriously.

* * * *

The next day dawned fair, but there were clouds on the horizon, which made the weather seem iffy. Howard and Elizabeth ate breakfast in the hotel's café. Stefan had said he might turn up to see them off, but failed to show up, and the day felt a little flatter as a result.

"I don't understand why you insist on bringing that briefcase," Elizabeth said.

"Look, I may be obliged to go on this trip, but I don't think anyone can oblige me to completely waste my time."

"I wonder where Stefan is," Elizabeth asked.

"Some co-ed's bed, no doubt," Howard said, dismissively. He opened his briefcase and was already absorbed in arranging it to his liking. "I suppose they will have lunch up there?" He actually was fully prepared for the group to be as flaky about this as their name implied, and had gotten up early and had the hotel make some sandwiches for him, which were now safely stowed away in his briefcase. If she behaved herself, he would share them with Elizabeth.

"I wouldn't worry about it," Elizabeth said. "Look, there's the bus now."

Howard had been afraid they would be condemned to some rickety van spouting noxious fumes for the journey, but no, it was a big luxury tourist coach. Somewhat to his surprise several other people sitting in the café got up and made their way toward the bus. Others joined them from the lobby. Howard surveyed the scene as he stood there waiting. Among them, two little old ladies, one fat, one thin, happily gossiping to themselves; a skinny Goth kid, who hung back sullenly smoking; a very earnest looking Englishwoman, who was either a serious academic or some daft birdwatcher (or both); and two young college age girls whom he immediately pegged as California New Age sun-worshippers, until he overheard them conversing in German. He groaned.

"What is it now, Howard?" Elizabeth asked, a little more impatiently than was her wont.

"Everyone getting on this bus is from the hotel."

"So?"

"Use your head, Elizabeth. Can't you see that it's a racket? The hotel delivers these fancy invitations, and in return they must get a cut of the profits."

"What profits?" Elizabeth asked with irritation. "It's a free tour, Howard."

"So you keep telling me."

She glared at him and then they followed the others into the bus. After a few moments, a dark haired young woman dashed rather breathlessly aboard. "Sorry I'm late, everyone. I'm Jennifer Brooks, and I'll be your guide to Lord Erdely's Castle today. I think we are all just going to have a fascinating time, and I hope you are looking forward to it as much as I am." She tapped the driver on the shoulder and made some quick hand motions to him, then handed him a piece of paper, which he studied intently.

He nodded.

"By the way, this is our driver, Vlad Mysecki. Vlad is deaf, so don't bother trying out your newfound Romanian phrases on him, okay?" She tapped Vlad on the shoulder again, and the bus started off.

Vlad managed to snake through the narrow streets of downtown Cornifu without too much trouble, but before long, there was a murmur from the little old ladies. Finally one of them raised her hand hesitantly, and said, "Excuse me, dear, but aren't we going the wrong way? I mean according to this map—"

"Terrific," Howard groaned. "We even have our own bloody Miss Marple aboard."

"Shh," Elizabeth said.

"I mean, does she really think they don't know the way to their own castle?"

"Oh, I apologize, Miss Erickson. We have one brief stop before we can head on up to Castle Erdely. It won't take long."

A sigh of impatience went through the bus and then subsided. Within a few blocks, the bus came to a sudden halt, and a new passenger leapt aboard. Or not so new—it was Stefan.

"Everyone, I'm delighted to welcome my good friend, Professor Stefan Petrescu. He will be accompanying us on our tour today, and I am sure he can enlighten us on the more historic aspects of the castle far better than I can." Jennifer beamed at him.

Stefan beamed back at her in turn.

"I think we can now begin to surmise what it was that detained him this morning," Howard said.

"Hush," Elizabeth said.

Stefan made his way back through the bus, and took a seat directly opposite Elizabeth's.

"Good morning, Howard. Good morning, Elizabeth. I hope you don't mind that I waggled an invitation to come along with you."

"Of course not," Elizabeth said. "But I believe that's 'wangled', Stefan, not waggled."

"I wouldn't be so sure about that, Lizzy," Howard said, sotto voce. "I bet I know just what it was he waggled."

* * * *

"So tell me, Professor Petrescu," said the British woman, who he had ended up next to. "Are you also a skeptic about the paranormal, as so many of us on the tour today seem to be?"

"I am not brave enough to be skeptical about the supernatural, Madame," he replied. "There it is," he continued.

Everyone moved over to his side of the bus to catch their first glimpse of the castle.

The day had been fair in the valley, but dark clouds hung over the mountains, framing the castle like a stage backdrop designed by an overdramatic set designer. The castle, perhaps benign enough in fair weather, took on a brooding aspect in the theatrical light. The tour group, which had been chatty on the way up, grew quiet, as everyone watched to see the castle appear again and again from different perspectives on the twisting mountain road.

At the moment they got their first full view of it, a bolt of lightning shot across the sky, followed immediately by a loud clap of thunder.

Everyone, with the exception of Howard, gasped.

"Lord Erdely's little joke," Jennifer Brooks said. There was nervous laughter.

"Oh, come on!" Howard said. "And you call yourself skeptics." He shook his head. It was looking to be a long day.

* * * *

Vlad pulled the bus into a small graveled parking area and stopped. As they all made their way off the bus and stood stretching and gazing at the castle, a few plump raindrops fell.

"Hope no one was counting on a picnic," Howard said, with malicious glee. He detested picnics. The last thing he'd wanted to do today was to sit cross-legged out in the middle of some field, gulping down food before the ants could act on their invasion plans.

"Oh, don't worry, Professor Green," Jennifer said. "We'll have a lovely meal all set out for you in the dining room. We'll serve that at noon, and then begin the official tour when we're done." She glanced involuntarily at Stefan.

Howard gloated at the confirmation of his suspicions.

"Anyway, I'll just start heating things up. Meanwhile, why don't you all just have a look around before we eat?"

Elizabeth watched the young woman struggle forward with her parcels. "Can I help?" she asked.

"Oh, no," Jennifer said. "This stuff is all microwavable." She smiled at Elizabeth's surprise. "What? You were expecting cooking over an open-fireplace, maybe? No, we're showing you Lord Erdely's castle today, not forcing you to live his lifestyle."

Elizabeth caught a glimpse of a very modern kitchen before Jennifer shooed her cheerfully away.

The others had wandered into the older part of the house in the meantime. Howard and Stefan were standing in a room full of old portraits.

"I could see you dressed in something like that, Stefan," Howard was saying, as he stared at the image of a grave young man in velvet, with a golden chain around his neck, a tam of some kind set rakishly on his head, and a stunning hawk perched silently and somewhat menacingly on his arm, as if it were only waiting for a signal to be set forth on some nefarious mission. "He even looks like you a little."

"Oh, I wouldn't doubt it," Stefan said. "My family has been here for centuries. Just by the odds, he's bound to be a relative of some kind. I like to think I have a better attitude than this fellow does, though." But he stared pensively at the portrait, and the gravity of his expression matched the portrait sitter's own. "Hello, Elizabeth," he said, sensing her approach, and breaking his trance to greet her.

"What do you think, Lizzie?" Howard asked with a smirk. "Should Stefan get himself a hawk like this fellow here, as, you know, sort of a fashion accessory? I really think he could pull it off."

There was a small, startled shriek from the adjoining room.

The threesome looked apprehensively at each other and then walked swiftly toward it.

But it was only the two German girls staring rather raptly at another large portrait.

"Is anything the matter?" Howard asked. He was not averse to comforting attractive young women when the need arose.

"Oh, no, *bitte*, no. We are only seeing the—what?" they consulted in rapid German "—the remarkable likeness to your wife."

Howard walked toward them and looked up and the others followed in his wake.

"Ach," said one of the girls, glancing from Elizabeth to the portrait and back again. "It is really quite astounding, this resemblance, yes?"

"Now, *frauleins*," Howard cajoled, "You've already been working yourself up a bit, haven't you? Seems as though you don't even need the haunted house tour they have all worked out for us to get your chills and thrills. You come all ready with your own self-induced shivers. No, it's a slight resemblance, nothing more. If you want to see a likeness, you should see this chap in the other room. Could be our Professor Petrescu's cousin. Come see what I mean."

And so saying, he put a hand on each girl's shoulder and herded them into the next room.

Elizabeth and Stefan watched him go, and then continued to regard the picture.

"What do you think? Shall I get myself a hawk?" Stefan asked, smiling to himself.

Elizabeth smiled, too.

* * * *

The tour itself was just gimmickry, as Howard had known it would be. All rumors and myths and unverified sightings. Still, he should probably be taking some notes. It might be fruitful to compare these undocumented tales with those circulating about other Transylvanian castles. No doubt some common themes would emerge and new cultural insight be given. A myth like Dracula—or Lord Erdely—didn't just spring from nowhere. There were reasons—not the reasons the peasants thought there were, but there were always reasons for such legends. Political, economic reasons. All you had to do was trace it back.

Tedious, though. What he really needed right now was a good nap.

As that didn't seem to be an option, he hung back with the German girls, who, like Howard, had indulged in more than their fair share of the surprisingly good Transylvanian wine served earlier with lunch.

Elizabeth glanced back at him from time to time in what he took to be a disapproving fashion. *What?* He mouthed to her. He was enjoying himself.

Wasn't that exactly what she'd been asking of him the whole time? Now here he was giving himself over to it, and apparently he was having too good a time. There was just no pleasing some people.

He stopped to gaze out of one of the narrow windows they passed. Boy, it was really coming down out there.

* * * *

The German girls had finally extricated themselves from his company, apparently more interested in the taciturn Goth, who had also hung back from the group, though merely to sneak another cigarette here and there. If this castle had been a real antiquity, Howard would have been enraged that the boy had simply ignored the 'Smoking Strictly Forbidden' signs, printed in several major languages. As it was, he felt for the kid. It had been an awfully long tour. But at last it was over.

As he came down the great staircase to rejoin the others in the lobby he thought, *at least now I'll be allowed to continue with my own plans*. There was a limit to how much obstruction he was prepared to politely put up with. He supposed that he would find Elizabeth sulking a little at his non-participation in the tour of this ersatz castle, and wasn't looking forward to facing her. Well, he would tell her it was a matter of principle.

Fortified, he glanced down at her in the castle's massive foyer, where he was slightly surprised to find her chatting animatedly with Stefan. *Good old Stefan*, Howard thought, suddenly fond. Trust him to keep the ladies entertained.

When he descended into the foyer, though, he immediately sensed a new air of anxiety in the group.

"What's up?" he asked Elizabeth, walking up to her. Stefan seemed to have disappeared for the moment.

"Vlad came in and signed to Jennifer that the storm has brought a tree down over the road. We can't leave," Elizabeth said.

"Can't leave? What do you mean, can't leave?"

"Howard," Elizabeth said with some exasperation, "What do you think I mean by *can't leave?*"

"But I mean, for how long?"

"I don't know. That's what Jennifer is trying to find out now. Apparently, the phone lines have gone down, too. She's gone up to the castle ramparts to see if she can get any cell phone reception up there. Stefan is going to go up to see what she's found out."

So here's where the scam begins, Howard thought. *They'll probably make us ante up some exorbitant amount just to get the tree cutters up here, and meanwhile, we don't know that there's even a tree at all!*

"Just where is this tree?" he asked.

"For heaven's sake, Howard, what does it matter where the tree is?"

"How did Vlad find out about it? I mean, it's not like he was whiling away the hours listening to the radio, now is it?"

Stefan made his way back to them. "Jennifer can't get any cell phone reception right now either. What's the problem, Howard?"

"I think I would just like to have a little proof that this tree that's fallen on the road actually exists before I blindly submit to whatever extortion this so-called paranormal society has in mind for us."

Stefan eyed him coolly. "You are very savvy, Howard. Very much a Yankee, I think."

"Well, thank you," Howard said. But he was confused. Stefan's words were gracious, but his tone seemed a bit chilly.

"Vlad indicated that it was just down the road," Elizabeth said. "It must be right on the property. I expect that's how he knew."

"Fine. Let's go take a look."

"What is the point of this, if I may ask?" Stefan inquired.

"Well, no offense, Stefan, but your countrymen do seem to let themselves be flummoxed by every little minor setback. First it was the library, where it would only have been a simple matter of unwrapping a bit of plastic to have access to the manuscripts, and now this. Maybe what's called for is just a little, well, yes—Yankee ingenuity, since you brought it up. It might turn out to be more of a branch than a tree—something we could hack through ourselves rather than waiting for some Romanian civil servant to show up."

Stefan turned and looked out the window for a while. "It is raining very hard," he said. "Coming down in buckets, do you say?" he asked, turning to Howard.

"A little rain never hurt anyone," Howard said, stubbornly.

"As you wish, Howard," Stefan said. "We shall visit the tree."

* * * *

The outing to the tree had a surprising number of takers—perhaps because there was really nothing much else to do until help arrived. Jennifer stayed back to see what could be done about accommodating everyone overnight, and some, including Elizabeth, opted to stay and build a warm fire, but a motley crew in a variety of thrown-together raingear followed Vlad out into the storm.

He faced the storm a little grimly, looking like an Old Testament prophet, but then perhaps battling the elements gave all their faces that stoic set. Still, it was an adventure, and Howard realized he was even a little bit excited by the prospect.

Though it seemed to take an age to get there, the fallen tree was, in fact, not very far—just past the first bend and then down the road a hundred yards. Even from a distance it was clear that it was enormous. Still, having set out, they all decided to try to reach it anyway, as a point of honor.

"So you see, Howard," Stefan said, "this is not a matter for Yankee ingenuity. It is a matter for a Romanian crane."

At least that, Howard thought despondently. *We'll be lucky to be out of here within the week.*

The German girls had run on ahead, and now stood giggling and shrieking atop the broad girth of the fallen tree.

The Goth boy took pictures of them with his cell phone.

The British woman strolled forward, too, and soon everyone was taking everyone else's picture at the site of their calamity.

As Howard and Stefan consented to be photographed together, Howard said, "So what's the truth behind all this Lord Erdely nonsense? Was he as wicked as everyone says?"

"What is truth, my friend?" Stefan shrugged. "I am afraid there is not all that much that would hold up to your rigorous methods of inquiry, Howard." But he said this with just the slightest hint of mockery in his voice.

"But this Lord Erdely—did he even exist?"

"Oh, yes—he existed all right." Stefan hesitated. "As a matter of fact, I believe he may have been a relative." He smiled at Howard. "As for being the black sheep of the family, well, one can never tell whether someone has been unjustly maligned—isn't that so?"

* * * *

When they returned to the castle, Jennifer greeted them rather ruefully at the door. "I'm afraid the electricity has gone out now, too. I've been getting the candles out, and putting them in strategic places, but I suppose we'd better use them sparingly. After all, we don't really know how long we're going to be here." For the first time, she looked a little frightened.

Stefan took her hands in his. "Ah, our good Miss Brooks. Let us not worry just yet. After all, you have two Romanians here! Let us show you a little of our Romanian ingenuity!" He gave just the slightest wink at Howard, and then with a nod at Vlad to follow him, he left the room.

* * * *

Within the hour, and before night had well and truly fallen, a roaring fire blazed in the hearth. From the iron pot slung over it, came the savory smell of stew—partially out of cans, mixed with potatoes and carrots from the root cellar and some mysterious herb that none of the travelers could identify. A couple of bottles of Carpathian Red had been liberated from the wine cellar, and the consensus from the detained travelers was none of them really had all that much to complain about.

"While we're waiting for our meal," Jennifer said, "let's discuss the sleeping arrangements. We have room for most but not all in the refurbished faculty area. Since they're the only married couple with us this trip, I thought Professor and Mrs. Green might like the room we think may have been Lord Erdely's own. It's quite romantic—the bedstead has been carved from a single massive oak—probably a cousin of the very one that's delayed us today—and with a fire properly banked up, it's actually quite cozy."

"Well, I—" Howard began, not because he really saw any reason to complain, but just because he didn't like things decided for him.

"That will be fine." Elizabeth cut him off.

Howard started to protest, but a look from Elizabeth decided him against this.

"And then I thought Christina and Lotte could have that smaller room on the same hall. And—I'm sorry, what was your name again?" Jennifer asked the Goth.

"Laszlo," he said.

"That's funny, I don't recall any Laszlo—" She looked briefly at her roster. "Isn't your name Boyd? Boyd Jones?"

"Oh, if you want to keep calling me by my Christian name, fine," he sneered.

"Well, you'll be sleeping—"

"Whatever," he said, and went outside into the rain to smoke.

* * * *

"So I think that's everyone," she said at last.

"But you've forgotten Professor Petrescu," one of the little old ladies said.

"Oh, I have!" Jennifer said, flustered.

"Never mind, my dear. I shall just make myself comfortable here on the couch," Stefan said.

"I'll bet she hadn't," Howard whispered to his wife. "Forgotten, I mean. I'll bet she has a warm bed all lined up for him and hoping no one else would notice. Too bad Miss Marple's on the case."

"Howard, will you please keep your lascivious thoughts to yourself!" Elizabeth whispered back.

Although she might be waiting a long while, Howard reflected. *Those German girls seemed hot to trot, and why share a bed with one when you could share it with two? Speaking of which, where were they? Probably standing in the rain with that wretched boy. Boyd.* He snickered. *What a moniker.*

As if summoned, the German girls suddenly reappeared, their arms loaded with what appeared to be linens. "Look what we have found!" they said, triumphantly. They looked at each other, perplexed. "How do you call?" then it dawned on them as one: "Pajamas!"

They weren't really pajamas, Howard thought—more on the order of nightshirts and nightgowns, but they were certainly very fine. Very old, too, if he was any judge, though they didn't smell musty—quite the opposite, in fact. Must have been boxed up in something nice—cedar, maybe. He sighed. These were probably the only true historic relics in the castle, and here his fellow travelers were getting their grubby paws all over them.

The girls said there were some more old clothes, in particular some old gowns the women could wear for a change of clothes the next day. Howard hoped that maybe he could rescue a few of those before they came to harm.

The events of the day had been trying, and after their meal, everyone made ready to retire early. It was only as he was getting up to go to bed that Howard realized his briefcase was missing.

* * * *

After he'd had the whole group hunting for a good three quarters of an hour Elizabeth finally persuaded him to call the search off, saying they could all resume in the morning, when the light was better.

"Do you have any idea how important that briefcase is?" Howard asked disconsolately as they got into bed.

"Of course I know how important it is to you," she said.

Howard did not fail to detect the subtle change she had made to his phrasing.

"But it's not like it can have really gone anywhere, is it? It can't have just walked off the mountain all by itself."

"I'll bet that kid took it. That Boyd."

"Laszlo? What would he want with your old briefcase?"

"Took it just because he could, I'll bet," he said.

"Blow out the candle, Howard."

* * * *

He woke to find Elizabeth missing. Or, more accurately, he woke *because* Elizabeth was missing—because he had had the sensation of her leaving the bed, and it woke him.

He looked up and thought he saw the last of her white nightgown trailing out the door.

He rolled over. Normally, he would have fallen back to sleep again. But he was in a strange place, and sleep didn't come that easily. So he lay there waiting for her return.

After about ten minutes he began worrying. *She hasn't taken the candle*, he realized. *Making her way around this old pile without a light?* Well, that was just folly. Typical Lizzie.

He supposed it was up to him to rescue her. He groaned and got out of bed, bemoaning the fact that he had no slippers, and obliged to get out of bed at all. He walked down the hall calling out 'Elizabeth!' in a dramatic stage whisper, which he soon recognized to be both pointless and ridiculous.

A door creaked open slowly on its hinge, startling him.

He saw it swinging outward slightly and went toward it, peering in. Inside, he found the two German girls with that Boyd fellow, engaged in a convoluted sexual position he did not recall ever having heard tell of before, let alone witnessed.

One of the girls looked up and saw him standing there gaping. She smiled a little wickedly and beckoned him in.

Flattered but terrified, he shook his head, shut the door firmly and moved on. He could hear the sound of their mocking laughter behind him all the way down the hall. He felt old.

Worse than that, though, he was turned around. He couldn't remember where the bathroom was supposed to be, which was surely where Elizabeth was headed. Suddenly, here he was back in the living room again, the bright fire damped down a bit, and the couch—well, the couch was empty.

So Stefan had found another bed for the night, the rogue. He thought he could narrow down pretty well whose it was. He smiled appreciatively, feeling generous. After all, hadn't he been offered another bed tonight himself? So what if it was half in mockery?

He went on, passing the faculty sleeping area, sure that the bathroom must be around there somewhere. Wouldn't mind a whiz himself. He entered the old kitchen, and saw an open door leading into darkness. He seemed to recall Jennifer pointing it out earlier when they were getting the plates and silverware for dinner, so maybe this was where the bathroom was, though it seemed an awful long way to go for a pee. Whatever happened to the good old-fashioned chamber pot?

He walked through the door, only to hear it swing shut with a bang behind him.

Too late, he realized he had walked into the larder.

It was only after repeated yells and pounding he reluctantly resigned himself to the idea he'd be locked inside for the remainder of the night.

At around six, Howard awoke to the sound of the pantry door squeaking open. He looked up to see Vlad coming in, apparently getting some provisions for breakfast.

Vlad didn't seem terribly surprised to see Howard sitting there on the floor —resting his head rather gingerly against a shelf of canned vegetables, but Howard didn't think he looked particularly pleased about it either.

He smiled meekly and gratefully at Vlad, realizing at once that any attempt to explain himself would be futile. He got up and walked past Vlad with as much dignity as he could muster, then continued on his urgent quest for the bathroom, which he now discovered was very close to his bedroom, but in the entirely opposite direction.

Howard found Lizzie sleeping peacefully when he returned to their room. His joints stiff from his night's travails, he climbed rather clumsily into bed beside her and tugged the blankets toward his own side a little more sharply than he would have normally. But, after spending the night on a cold larder floor because he'd been worried enough to go looking for her, he wasn't all that concerned about waking her at this point.

"Howard?" she asked in a groggy voice. "Where have you been all night?"

"Where have I been? Where have you been?"

"Me? I've been right here."

"Not the whole time."

"Not the—well, I suppose I got up to use the bathroom once, but that's all."

"You were gone a long time."

"Was I? I don't remember. Not as long as you've been gone."

"That's because I was forced to spend my night in the larder."

"By whom?" she asked.

He wanted to blame someone—the German girls, or Laszlo/Boyd, even Stefan. But it wouldn't fly. "By myself, I suppose," he said glumly.

"Oh, Howard," she said, smiling at him with a look that was half sympathy and half scorn.

"Don't tell the others," he implored her.

* * * *

A subdued Howard spent most of the day apart. It was still raining out, though not heavily as it had been, and the younger people went out for a while. He didn't feel like joining them, or indeed, anybody else. He gave the excuse of needing to look for his briefcase, which he did, but half-heartedly didn't really expect to find it. Someone had taken it for their own purposes, that much he knew. Probably simple spite. If they were in a generous mood, they might give it back. Most likely it was lying at the bottom of some swamp behind the castle, he felt.

He would have expected to feel worse about that possibility than he did. His colleagues had ridiculed him for not bringing along his laptop, but, and this was rich given the circumstances, he had been afraid someone would steal it. He'd been carrying around the old briefcase since he was a graduate student, and it had felt like his talisman. Now taken from him, he simply felt defeated. Old, and defeated.

The German girls tired of fooling around in the rain and came back in to dry themselves by the fire. Having taken off their wet clothes, they reappeared in two of the old gowns they had found, and before long had cajoled Elizabeth and Jennifer into playing dress-up with them. The English woman, apparently skeptical about everything and not just the paranormal, watched them stonily, refusing to participate, and eventually went back to poring over the ancient Latin tomes she had found in the library.

The German girls first did each other's hair in an old-fashioned style, and then persuaded Elizabeth to let them do hers.

Their energy is boundless, Howard thought, watching them all for a while from an upper landing before resuming his quest. *Is it really just their youth that makes them so?*

Stefan came in and sat in one of the armchairs, watching the little scene pensively, although on the surface it wouldn't seem to warrant such a somber response.

Howard had the feeling Stefan knew that he was up there watching, but if so, he didn't acknowledge Howard's presence.

Jennifer tried her cell phone again that afternoon, and finally got some reception.

"They aren't going to be able to get to that tree for a couple of weeks," she said, to a chorus of groans. "But the good news is that they'll send another bus up as far as where the road meets the highway tomorrow morning. All we need to do is find a way to get around that tree. Of course some of us could climb over, but not everyone."

No, not everyone, Howard thought sadly. *I, for instance, couldn't do it anymore.* Though, before this trip, he admitted to himself, he might have tried.

"Don't forget, I hiked all around these parts as a boy. I can certainly find a path that will work for everyone," Stefan said.

"That's settled then," Jennifer said. We're rescued!"

"Hooray!" was the general cry, though Howard did not participate.

In good spirits now, they decided to eat at the banquet table and to make what feast they could.

At a certain hour the 'ladies' arose to dress for dinner, and even Stefan and Laszlo, participated, though Howard declined.

"Is something wrong with your husband?" Jennifer asked Elizabeth.

"He's just missing his briefcase," Elizabeth said.

Howard, overhearing this, tried to detect some ridicule in her voice, but she sounded quite compassionate. This was somehow worse.

It wasn't his briefcase he was missing—it was his sense of his life's purpose. Not even the complete recovery of all his field notes could now quite give that back to him.

* * * *

The women all looked lovely at dinner, but Elizabeth was radiantly so.

Howard, sitting across from her, thought that by candlelight, she did look a little like the woman in the portrait after all. Just a little. But then they all looked as though they could have been in that portrait gallery that evening. Stefan looked more like his long dead relative than ever, and even little Boyd Jones, having removed his piercings, looked like nothing so much as a page boy standing attendance, as he stood solemnly filling the old ladies' water glasses.

Howard felt a ghostly presence around the table, not a haunting so much as an interpenetration of two realms, the past and the present—as if the second was only a kind of overlay upon the first.

* * * *

The group had again retired early, but Howard woke up from deep sleep to find Elizabeth standing at the foot of the bed. She was still dressed in her party costume, even though it must be quite late. This puzzled him. He'd changed into his nightshirt hours ago.

"Howard," she whispered, though her voice sounded thick and unfamiliar.

She's had too much wine, he thought. *If she's been up all this time, she must have.*

She beckoned to him.

He continued to lie there staring at her, until amidst her garbled speech, he thought he heard the word 'briefcase'. "Come!" she said urgently. "Come!"

What a dear, loyal old thing she was after all, he thought, struggling into his shoes. (He wasn't going to make the mistake of wandering around barefoot again.) Here he'd been judging her for drinking, but all the while, she'd been toiling tirelessly on his behalf, and had apparently been successful where he had failed. It would be a shame to tell her that he lacked heart for the project now. Well, maybe he could summon it up again, once he had the briefcase back. For her sake.

Once they were out of the room, she moved quickly. She was more agile, sprier than Howard really thought of her as being, and he had to hurry to keep up. He thought he had pretty much covered all the territory for the day, but didn't recognize the rooms they were crossing now. Perhaps they just looked different in the moonlight.

Moonlight, he realized. It had finally stopped raining. He would have paused to look out at the lovely Carpathian Mountains in the moonlight if only he didn't have to expend every ounce of energy he had just to keep up.

Elizabeth's gait was odd, almost inhuman. If she had been an animal, he would have described it as 'loping'.

But now she was just ahead of him, climbing a steep, narrow staircase he was pretty certain he had never seen before.

The door at the top was small—too small for a modern day man to get through easily. She disappeared through it, and he followed on more slowly. *Enough,* he thought, stopping for a moment to catch his breath. *Even if I lose her now, enough.*

He reached the last step and peered into the room. On a table, by lamplight, sat the briefcase. He expected to see Elizabeth there, pointing at it proudly. But she was nowhere near it. Apart from the briefcase, the room seemed to be empty.

As his eyes grew more accustomed to the light, he startled to realize there was a couple standing in the corner, locked in amorous embrace. He caught a swift glimpse of the woman's profile. Elizabeth? And the man . . . but the man turned now and stared at him directly. Howard was still trying to decide whether this was the man in the portrait or whether it was Stefan—the eyes certainly seemed . . . but the man gave a low whistle, and the hawk, unseen until now, rose swiftly from its perch in the corner of the room. With a low swoop it came rapidly toward Howard. Whether it meant to hurt him or not, Howard would never know. He took a step back and pitched headlong down the staircase.

* * * *

"Howard? Howard?"

Angels, Howard thought. *So there really are angels.*

But then his focus returned and he spotted Elizabeth and Stefan hovering over him in their funny old white nightgowns. *Just a dream then*, Howard thought, *nothing to worry about at all.*

"Howard, you've taken a tumble, my friend," Stefan said. "How on earth did you get here? Are you all right?"

"Nothing to worry about at all," Howard said, aloud. Though he didn't know himself exactly how he'd come to be lying on the cold, stone floor. Had he been sleepwalking?

"Well, all the same, I think we'd better get someone to look at you. Luckily for us, that British woman, Emily Strickland, turns out to be a doctor."

"Good for her, good for her," Howard said. "Much better than being a skeptic."

It was only much later, after Doctor Strickland had looked him over and applied mustard plasters to all his little cuts and bruises that it occurred to him to wonder how Elizabeth and Stefan had managed to come across him together in such a remote corner of the house at that time of night. He was grateful, of course, but he couldn't quite manage to forget those nightgowns.

* * * *

As they wended their way down the trail from Lord Erdely's Castle to the roadside the next day, Howard kept fancying he was one of the children in *The Sound of Music*—perhaps Friedrich. He hummed a few bars of the title song as he walked. From time to time, he managed to be of aid to the two little old ladies cheerfully struggling on just ahead of him, but he never really took his eyes off Stephan, who lead them all back to 'safety'. Howard liked pretending he was one of the stalwart children, but every once in a while it crossed his mind that what he would really like to be was one of the Nazis, with a pistol aimed right at Baron von Trapp's head. One thing was certain—at this range, he wouldn't miss.

Finally, they reached the highway. Jennifer was in cell phone contact with the van arriving to pick them up shortly. The others were chattering excitedly about having reached 'civilization,' even though this was nothing more than a lonely patch of Carpathian highway.

Stefan came up to Howard, and opening up the bundle he had been carrying under his arm, rather sheepishly handed Howard's briefcase back to him. Howard took it without expression.

"You knew I had it, didn't you?" Stefan asked.

"Not at first," Howard admitted. "But, yes, in the end, I did." He shook it. He could hear his papers rustling inside. "Is it all there?"

"Almost all. I threw out those sandwiches you were hoarding. They were starting to get moldy."

"Ah," Howard said. He was well past the point of being embarrassed before Stefan. "Why did you take it?"

"Because I needed to see what you were working on, Howard. What you were saying about my home. About my people."

"I'm a scholar, Stefan. Why would you worry about that?"

"Because of what you were saying when you were not being a scholar."

"And what was your conclusion? What would you suggest?"

Stefan looked at him solemnly. "Begin again."

"Thanks," Howard said tightly. "I'll keep your advice in mind. Well, I suppose we should shake hands or something." He extended it. Stefan took it a little tentatively.

"There's something else."

Now we get to it, Howard thought. "Yes?"

"I—we—Elizabeth and I are not coming back with you."

"Really?" he asked, trying for surprise. It came out flatly. He had suspected as much.

"Yes."

"Not even down to Cornifu?"

"No, not for a while, anyway."

"Let me ask you something—how long has this been going on between you two? Just since the beginning of this trip? Or longer?"

"Since the first night I was invited to your house for dinner," Stefan said. "But for me, well, truthfully, it was even before that."

"Now you finally surprise me," Howard said. "How is that?"

"I told you I had been in the castle before the Paranormal Association took over. It was run down, but much of it was the same as it is now, just less well tended. I had often stopped and marveled at the picture that so resembles your wife. The other boys used to make fun of me, saying I had fallen in love with a dead woman. I scoffed at that, but in a way, it was true—I had. Naturally, I found out what I could about her. She was called Elizabeta Roman, and she lived in Lord Erdely's time. That much is known. The rest is legend. I will tell you the legend, if you like. "

"Please."

"Elizabeta was of the nobility, but Erdely is said to have abducted her as a young girl and treated her like a servant. In other words, she kept the company of servants, and so it is not surprising that she found some solace in one Radu Petrescu, who was Lord Erdely's Master of Hawks. Also quite possibly Erdely's illegitimate relation, perhaps even a brother.

"When Erdely found out about their love for each other, he instructed Radu to take her to the ramparts and set his hawk on her. To blind her—you understand? But Radu wouldn't. He freed the hawk and leapt from the ramparts instead. Erdely caught Elizabeta before she could jump, too. He blinded her anyway—without Radu's help."

"Very tragic. Only a legend, though—you said as much yourself."

"But things live on in legends, don't they? Sometimes legend is the only life they have. Despite all your scholarship, that's something you haven't really understood yet, Howard. But Elizabeth—our Elizabeth—did."

On hearing her name, Elizabeth, who had been talking with the others, now made her way over. Howard couldn't help noticing she looked younger than ever.

"He told me about the resemblance when we first met, of course," she said. "From then on, I was determined to see her. Elizabeta. I've been researching Cornifu and Lord Erdely's legend since the day I met Stefan." She looked at Howard squarely. "I suppose it was because of her that we really became friends."

"Friends. So that's what you call it."

"It's what I called it then. It isn't what I'd call it now."

Stefan slipped his arm around her waist.

"You've fallen in love with him, then?"

She said nothing.

"I guess it's not surprising that you found him more interesting." Howard couldn't entirely suppress a note of self-pity.

"No, Howard. I found him more interested in me."

Howard stood mulling it all over. Finally he said, "There never was any notable collection in Cornifu, was there?"

"No," Stefan said. He had the grace to be embarrassed. "My friend is the head of the library. I asked him to close it down for a month. I have to say, he leapt at the chance. He's off hiking in Turkey. He'll come back, splash on a new coat of paint before he opens it again. No one will be the wiser."

"Unless I tell them. He could lose his job."

"But you won't, will you?" Stefan said. "You can't really wish to harm a person you've never even met."

"Oh, I don't know about that. God knows, I'd like to harm someone."

"Me, then," Stefan said, stepping up to him. "No other. Only me."

Howard looked at Stefan as if he would indeed be only too happy to punch him. But in the end he let his clenched fists slacken. He turned to Elizabeth. "How could you use my interest in the Carpathians and turn it all against me like this?"

"Howard, you had no interest at all in this region until I started talking it up a bit. It was my ancestry, not yours, remember?"

"That's true." Elizabeth Green, nee Dodrescu. It was beginning to dawn on him just how little that had happened in recent months had been precisely what it seemed. "So what will you do now?"

"We are going to go back to the castle and see if we can lay to rest the ghosts of Elizabeta and Radu," Stefan said. "You saw them the night you fell, didn't you, Howard?"

Howard hesitated. He still wasn't entirely sure what he'd seen. But in the end he nodded. Ghosts were as good an explanation as any.

"We don't know if we can, of course." Stefan went on. "But we feel we must try."

"Well, good luck with that," Howard said. He even thought he meant it, mostly.

There was a honk from far down below, and a little van could be seen struggling valiantly up the mountain.

"There's my ride. I guess I'd better make a move." He stood there a moment and then embraced his wife, kissing her on the cheek. Impulsively, he kissed Stefan on the cheek, too. Then he turned and started down the hillside.

"Begin again, Howard," Stephan called out rather sternly after him.

Doesn't look like I have much choice about that, Howard thought bleakly. He looked at the battered old briefcase in his hand, emblematic of so much of his scholarly life, and suddenly grimaced. Then, putting the whole of his being into the action, he flung it out over the heavily wooded canyon on his right. He watched it disappear into the foliage and immediately felt better. Dazed and grinning, he turned back to see what Elizabeth and Stefan thought of his rash action.

But they had already disappeared.

AUTHOR'S BIO: Seana Graham is a bookseller at a large independent bookstore in Santa Cruz, California. Her short stories have appeared in a variety of magazines and literary journals. Her story "The Pirate's True Love" was recently anthologized in *The Best of Lady Churchill's Rosebud Wristlet,* and her story "Marina" was granted the *Zone 3* fiction award . She has also co-authored a trivia book on Southern California with Lisa Wojna for Blue Bike Press. She is very excited about having had this opportunity to try her hand at horror.

Hear No Evil, Speak No Evil
By
Donna Amato

"I am not going on this haunted castle tour, Dani!" Parker stated, with absolute finality.

"That's fine, I'll go by myself."

"You know how I hate stuff like that. It gives me the creeps," he continued, trying to convince himself more than Dani.

"I said it was fine, Parker. Just because we work together doesn't mean you have to follow me everywhere I go."

"You say that, but then you give me that look!"

"What look?"

Dani Jamison knew very well the look he was talking about. He had been the photographer for her travel articles for the last two years and that look had been there all along. She rolled her eyes, bit her bottom lip, and stared him down until he could do nothing but give in. She did it now.

Dani knew he would eventually agree and go with her. He always did. It was kind of a game between them. She asked, he said no, she gave the look, whatever that was, and he agreed.

"I hate when you do that!" Parker shouted, more frustrated with himself than her.

"What?"

"Okay, Okay, I'll go!" he said, completely disgusted with himself.

"It'll be fun, you'll see, and it's a good chance for me to gather some information for my mystery stories. You can get some great shots of the castle, too."

The tour would be great. She and Parker neared the end of their research for her article on travel in Transylvania and deserved a little time to relax. Parker got some great shots of the town of Cornifu, its tourist attractions and the mountains that stretched out behind it. Pictures of the castle would be an added bonus.

Later, alone in her hotel room, Dani glanced out the window and admired the town. The old stone buildings would draw anyone's attention, their majestic peaks spiraling into the sky. She enjoyed the local hotel. Old like the town, it was the perfect place to stay if you wanted to get the feeling of going back in time.

Glancing around her room she fully appreciated the elegance of the décor. She walked over to the ornate dresser, picked up the letter that had arrived earlier that morning and read it again.

Dear Miss Jamison:

We cordially invite you for a free tour within the famous castle of Lord Erdely.

Our guide, Jennifer Brooks, will be departing tomorrow at 8am sharp from the Hotel Cornifu for this one day excursion we have planned.

Visit the mysterious surroundings of the Erdely Castle and see for yourself if it is indeed haunted.

Yours truly,
Bruce Campbell
President of The American Paranormal Association of World Tours.

Parker had received the same letter and she suspected more of the Hotel Cornifu occupants had, as well. It was probably some promotional thing to get tourists to visit the castle, but Dani didn't mind.

She looked at her reflection in the mirror.

"You are such a liar, Dani Jamison. You know darn good and well why you want to go see this castle and it has nothing to do with some dumb travel article," she said aloud to herself. Her fascination with Nancy Drew stories started as a young girl. She'd outgrown the books but not her love of a good mystery.

* * * *

Early the next morning Dani and Parker found themselves waiting in the lobby with a group of hotel residents. For the most part they looked like your average tourist group ready to embark on a day excursion into town. They held quiet conversations in small groups while they waited for the tour bus to pick them up.

"Thanks for coming with me Parker."

"Sure, no problem."

"You're not scared are you?" she teased.

"No, I'm not scared. Places like that just freak me out. They're usually dark, damp, and full of cobwebs filled with the creatures that spin them."

"Oh, so it's not the ghosts you're afraid of, it's the spiders!"

"I don't believe in that haunted castle nonsense any more than you do, Dani."

As it got closer to the arrival time of the tour bus, the group moved outside to the stone driveway to await its arrival. The crisp fall air surrounded them. Within a short while, a bus rambled up the driveway and screeched to a halt in front of them. The doors opened and a young woman with brown, shoulder length hair descended the stairs. As soon as she addressed them, it became apparent she was American.

"Hello everyone, my name is Jennifer Brooks and I'll be your tour guide for today. You'll find the accommodations very comfortable for our trip."

Jennifer made a quick head count and by the smile spreading over her face, she seemed pleased with the turnout. She glanced at her watch then directed her attention back to the group.

"Thank you everyone for being on time. Now, if you will all board the bus we can be on our way." With that said, she climbed the stairs and took her seat behind the bus driver, a quiet man, who sat staring out the front window waiting for his cue to begin.

One by one they boarded and selected their seats. Dani managed to get the seat across the aisle from Jennifer. She planned to find out all she could on their ride to the castle. Parker, sitting in the seat directly behind Dani, found himself sandwiched between a quiet guy holding an overnight bag, and a busty blonde who chattered nonstop.

Trying to avoid forty-five minutes of unending dribble, Parker attempted to strike up a conversation with the bag clutcher.

"Hi, I'm Parker Connelly."

"James Dinmore." The man scooted closer to the window and peered out as though hoping that would be the end of the conversation.

"I thought this was a day trip. What's with the bag?" Parker motioned to the brown satchel sitting precariously on the man's lap.

Trying to ignore him, James clutched the bag until his knuckles turned white. He stared out the window, pretending to study the patterns of leaves on the ground below. The only indication he heard Parker at all was his death grip tightening on the bag every time Parker said something.

"Kassandra Cross," said the blonde to his left, extending her hand to him.

"Parker Connelly," he volunteered reluctantly, hoping that would be the end of it. He wasn't that lucky.

"Are you alone on this tour?" She leaned over the seat in his direction, her ample bosom almost falling out of the scrap of material she considered a shirt.

Taken off guard, Parker hesitated just long enough to hear James snicker behind him.

"I'm with her," he answered pointing in Dani's direction, never taking his eyes off the blonde's chest.

"I'm an actress. Maybe you've seen me? My last film was *Deep, Dark Secrets.*"

"No, can't say that I've seen it." He managed to drag his eyes up to her face. She was pretty, but he could tell some work had been done to make her appear younger than she was.

"What about *Into the Deep*? I was in that one, also."

"Nope, it doesn't ring a bell either." Parker hoped she would get tired of talking to him and turn to the other guy unfortunate enough to share a seat with her. That would be something to see. The guy was a nerd if ever he saw one, the total opposite of what Kassandra represented. He looked like a professor with his dark rimmed glasses that kept sliding down his nose, and if Parker wasn't mistaken, a plastic pocket protector peeked out from his coat, complete with pens. He sat quietly listening to their conversation.

"This is Hiram Banks," she said, introducing them. "We met while waiting in the lobby."

Hiram timidly offered his hand to Parker, blushing when his arm brushed against the starlet's attributes.

The doors closed, the bus lurched forward, and they were on their way.

They traveled through the town of Cornifu admiring the old world charm that made it unique. The fall leaves added to the picturesque landscape. As they reached the edge of town, Jennifer picked up the small microphone at her side and addressed the group.

"Welcome to the American Paranormal Association of World Tours. We embark today on a tour of the famous Erdely Castle. Lord John Erdely owned the castle, nestled deep in the Carpathian Mountains." Jennifer continued with the background of the Castle and Lord Erdely, capturing everyone's attention. "We'll spend our day touring the castle and grounds. I will be happy to answer questions, however, as I have explained, there really isn't that much information on Lord Erdely. We hope you enjoy the tour."

Dani listened to Jennifer intently. As a journalist, she knew there was always a story behind the story and she intended to find out what the real story was.

As the bus got farther from the town of Cornifu, they rode through thick trees adorned with the red, gold and brown leaves one would expect to see this time of year. They steadily ascended the mountain and could see the town growing smaller below them with each passing mile. Above them, a dense layer of fog stretched across the Carpathian Mountain peaks.

Eventually they turned onto a private road that wound itself through the trees. Dani could tell they were approaching the castle when the road turned to stone and the bus began bumping along its length.

They passed through a large iron gate… and there it was.

Her first glimpse of Erdely Castle caused butterflies to take flight in her stomach. She saw its massive peaks towering over the dense forest below. It appeared as though not much had changed since its original owner graced the halls. That thought made the hair on the back of her neck stand on end. Everyone on the bus sat silently, watching the castle get nearer and nearer.

Once the bus came to a halt, they disembarked and stood in a line facing the massive arched entryway. Stone steps lead up to the entrance and Jennifer climbed up several of them before turning to address the group.

"As you will notice, we have left the castle in as much of its original state as possible. There has been some addition of electricity to the lower level where the kitchen, dining area and restrooms are located, but even that has been well hidden to blend with the original look. The upper floors have no electricity or modern conveniences. The Association takes care of the upkeep and the kitchen is stocked with supplies for when the groundskeepers, maintenance crews and guests are here. Today we will be on our own though, undisturbed to explore as we wish. If you will please follow me inside, our adventure will begin."

Parker started snapping pictures with his digital camera as soon as he got off the bus. He stayed near Dani, and to his disgust, Kassandra and Hiram seemed intent on staying near him also. He heard the blonde talking non-stop right behind him.

"This is perfect!" She clapped her hands. "This is the perfect setting to get in character for my new movie, *Castle of Love*."

No one said anything because they didn't want to encourage her, but that didn't stop her.

"You don't mind if we tag along with you do you Parker?" she asked, pointing to Hiram.

Parker glanced her way, shrugged his shoulders and continued snapping photos.

They followed Jennifer through the doorway and into the main entrance. The massive entrance hall contained shining knights' armor, standing at the ready. They lined the hall on both sides. Huge paintings and tapestries adorned the walls, intermingled with wall sconces, their candles flickering with the draft from the doors.

Hallways darted off the main hall in different directions, tunnels beckoning to be explored.

Dani let her eyes follow the massive staircase as it climbed up the stone wall to the right. A smaller staircase branched off to the second floor and another to the third level. She couldn't wait to get up there and poke around on her own.

"I will take you on a tour of the bottom floor and inner courtyard. You will then have time to go exploring on your own. All I ask is that everyone meet in the main hall by five so we can return to the hotel."

They walked down one of the halls to a beautiful inner courtyard. There was a stone patio with several small round tables. Plants of every kind imaginable adorned the low stone walls surrounding the courtyard.

Dani and Parker looked up at the darkening sky. They noticed Jennifer looking at the clouds, also. Dampness suddenly filled the air, leaving a mist on the tables and chairs.

"This weather is going to wreck my hair." Kassandra ran her hands through the bleached blonde locks.

Parker shook his head and snapped a picture of Dani standing next to the stone wall. The blonde's voice raked on his nerves, which were already on edge. Why couldn't she just stop talking for a while?

Next, they stopped in the kitchen. It appeared more modern than the rest of the castle and well stocked. Tucked off to the side, it didn't distract from the look of the castle. The large dining room contained a long table made of dark wood. Surrounding chairs, with intricately carved backs and legs, completed the set. Ornate side tables lined the wall, candelabras adorning them. The room exuded elegance.

"There are sandwiches, cold salads, and drinks available for lunch today. You may help yourself whenever you are ready to eat," Jennifer informed them as she led the group from the dining area.

"The rest of the afternoon you are free to explore on your own. I'll be available here or in the dining area if you need me or have any questions. Enjoy yourselves, but please be back here by five so we can leave."

The group dispersed heading off in different directions. Dani grabbed Parker by the arm and headed for the stairs.

"Let's go to the second floor and see what we can find." She was unable to hide the excitement in her voice.

"I don't want to find anything!"

"This is supposed to be fun, Parker—you look like I'm leading you to be tortured."

Looking over his shoulder at Kassandra, who followed them, Hiram in tow, he shook his head.

"Aren't *you*?" he asked.

They both laughed, which lightened the mood until Kassandra's high pitched squeal joined in as she worked her way up the stairs on high heels not made for stone steps.

Hiram shook loose from her grasp and approached Parker and Dani.

"I'm sorry if we've intruded."

"It's okay," Dani answered, glancing back at Kassandra "You're welcome to join us if you can keep up. We have a lot to see and not much time."

They reached the second floor. It had a large, wide hallway lit with candles. There were more suits of armor, their blank stares more sinister in the dim lighting of the hall. Paintings graced the walls, intermingled with more swords than they could count.

"Stand by the armor Dani so I can get a picture," Parker said.

She stopped only long enough to pose for him to snap the picture then headed for the first door.

Parker looked at the photo displayed on his digital camera. Dani's smiling face stared back at him. She ate up the camera like she always did. Zooming it in a little closer, he noticed a dark spot over her right shoulder. He glanced at the area where they had taken the shot expecting to see the mark on the wall near the suit of armor. There wasn't anything there. He clicked back to the previous image of the hallway thinking there was something on the lens that had ruined all his shots. It was fine. He continued clicking back to check the other shots he'd taken since they got there. All the ones with Dani in them had the same dark spot poised over her right shoulder. Parker tried zooming in on the area but it just got blurry.

"Parker, you have to come in here and see this," Dani yelled.

He entered to find her sitting on a massive canopied bed that dominated the room. Detailed carvings covered every inch of it. Long, red velvet drapes hung from the window, blocking out any light that may have found its way into the room.

"Isn't this bed great?"

"No, it's scary looking. How in the world did you get up there?"

"The stepstool." She pointed to the side of the bed.

Parker looked, but there was nothing there.

"What stepstool?"

"That one right there, silly." She looked over the side of the bed to find nothing there.

Glancing back at Parker, she shook her head. "It was there, I swear to you."

Their two uninvited guests joined them. Kassandra went to the window and threw open the heavy drapes.

"Look, it's really raining out there."

Rain splashed against the window while a roll of thunder rumbled in the distance.

"Take my picture, Parker." Dani lay across the bed.

He took the picture, looking at it immediately. The same image was present over her shoulder.

"You need to look at something, Dani." Parker helped her off the bed.

Turning to head toward the hall where the light was better, Dani caught a glimpse of eyes peering at them through the crack of the bedroom door.

Parker almost ran into her back when she stopped short, her hand flying to her mouth to muffle a scream.

Recognizing James still clutching his bag, they moved forward to confront him. By the time they got to the hall, he had vanished.

"Where did he go?" asked Hiram.

"I have no idea, but I want you guys to look at something." Parker put a note of urgency in his tone.

Holding the camera out for them to see, he clicked through the pictures, one by one, waiting to see if they would notice anything.

"There must be something on the lens. Some of the pictures have smudges on them." Kassandra leaned in for a better look.

"That's what I thought at first, but it only appears in the shots with Dani in them. Something isn't right."

"Don't let your imagination run wild, Parker," Dani said. "It's probably just the bad lighting in this place," She smiled at what he'd implied. "Let's get on with our exploration."

The four of them checked out a few more rooms on the second floor.

Most of the bedrooms were mirror images of each other; dark furniture with storage areas. They took the stairs again and went up to the third floor. There they found more bedrooms and sitting areas. Dani thoroughly enjoyed herself checking out the rooms, opening doors and peeking inside.

At the end of the hallway they came to a locked door. Hiram tried unsuccessfully to open it for her.

"It won't budge, sorry."

"I'll have to remember to ask Jennifer about it. Thank you for trying."

Even from this floor they could hear the rain pounding against the roof. It was coming down in torrents now. Every so often, lightning flashed in the windows illuminating areas of the hallway and rooms as they explored.

"Lets go downstairs and grab a bite to eat before it's time to leave," Parker said.

Heading toward the stairs, they heard the creak of a door slowly opening. As they turned to see where the noise came from, the sound of a door slamming shut filled the hall.

Everyone jumped.

Dani could have sworn the sound came from the direction of the locked room. Glancing that way, she saw a flicker of light shine from beneath the doorway.

Hiram and Kassandra burst out laughing. Parker smiled but didn't join in. Dani was shaken but she laughed along with them.

"We're all letting this creepy castle get the best of us," she said.

They went down to the kitchen, chose what they wanted to eat, and carried it into the dining room, taking seats at the long table.

The group ate in companionable silence. They couldn't help but notice when James entered the room juggling a sandwich and drink in one hand while carrying his bag in the other.

He glanced down the length of the table and chose a place farthest away from them. Literally dropping his meal on the table because he refused to put the bag down, James sat, placed the bag in his lap and proceeded to eat.

"What a weirdo!" exclaimed Hiram, fingering the pens in his shirt pocket then sliding his glasses back up his nose.

Dani and Parker looked at each other and grinned.

"It's almost five." Parker glanced at his watch. "We'd better head to the entrance hall to meet Jennifer."

"I'm going to the little girl's room. Anybody want to come with me?" Kassandra directed her question toward Dani.

"No, that's okay, I'm good."

"Suit yourself!"

It looked as though most of the guests were already assembled in the main hall when they arrived. Jennifer did a quick head count.

"We're missing someone."

"Kassandra went to the ladies room," Hiram said.

"Okay. Well I have a bit of unsettling news. Due to the rain, the bus driver cannot get back up the mountain to pick us up. I have been on my cell phone talking to Bruce, the president of the tour company. Until the rain stops and the bus can return, we'll have to stay here—maybe a couple of nights. I know this is an inconvenience for everyone but it can't be helped. There are more than enough bedrooms upstairs to accommodate everyone and the kitchen is well stocked so we should be very comfortable. All of the beds have fresh linens and the fireplaces have been set up in case we need them for warmth. I will keep everyone posted on any new developments. Are there any questions?"

"Do we choose our own rooms or will they be assigned?" Dani asked.

"Everyone can pick their own rooms. A few of you may have to go to the third floor if we run out of space on the second, but they're all very comfortable."

The group dispersed and headed for the stairs. Dani and Parker followed the others, Hiram not far behind them.

"Someone should let Kassandra know what's going on." Hiram looked at Dani.

"I'll go tell her." Dani was not at all thrilled to have the task. She wanted to get upstairs and find her accommodations.

"I'll wait here for you, Dani. I want to make sure we get rooms next to each other," Parker said.

"Okay, I'll be right back."

Dani went into the ladies room, but no one was in there. She checked the dining area. Kassandra wasn't there either. As she headed back to the main hall she ran across Jennifer.

"I've been looking for Miss Cross and can't seem to find her. She has no clue we're to stay here."

"I'll take care of that for you. I'll make sure she's informed," Jennifer said.

"Thank you. Oh, there is a room on the third floor that's locked. Do you know why that is? "

"There shouldn't be any rooms locked that I know of, but it's possible maintenance may have locked it for some reason while working in the castle. That area used to be the servants quarters but they've recently been remodeled so we can use them for guests."

"Well someone left a light on in there. I could see it under the door."

"There isn't any electricity up there."

"The maintenance people must have left candles burning then. I definitely saw a light under the door."

"That really isn't possible. The maintenance crew hasn't been here for three days. Any candles would have burned out long ago. Maybe you just thought you saw a light."

"Maybe so," Dani answered reluctantly. She knew very well she had seen a light under that door but she wasn't going to argue the fact.

"If that's all you need," Jennifer said, "I have some things to take care of for the others."

Dani found Parker and Hiram waiting for her when she reached the main hall.

"I couldn't find Kassandra but Miss Brooks is going to look for her and let her know we're staying the night. Let's go."

Checking the second floor, they found only one room free.

"I'll take this one," Hiram said.

"We'll meet you later for dinner," Dani said.

After climbing the stone steps, Dani and Parker reached the third floor landing.

"This floor seems more deserted." An unexpected chill raced up Parker's spine. He turned, half expecting someone to be standing behind him. There was no one.

"Good, we shouldn't have any trouble finding rooms then."

Parker knocked on doors, checking to see if any were occupied. It didn't take him long to find two empty rooms next to each other.

"I feel better knowing that I'll be close by if you need me," he said.

"Thanks, I'll meet you in about an hour to go for dinner." Dani touched his arm. She could feel how tense he was and looked up at him.

"You okay?"

"I'll be fine. Yell if you need me."

Dani shivered in the darkness once she stepped into her room. The setting sun made eerie shadows dance over the walls.

She lit the oil lamp and watched it cast a welcoming glow around her. It was a nice space, not as big as rooms downstairs, but comfortable.

Walking around she let her hand slide over the surface of the armoire, her fingers enjoying the nicks and gouges of its weathered surface. In the corner to the right was a nice size couch with the same dark covering that adorned the windows. She glanced at the large inviting bed.

Ignoring the urge to spread out in its center, she chose instead to go exploring.

Cracking the door, she peeked out to see if anyone was there.

Seeing no one, she ventured into the hall, stopping abruptly when she sensed a presence near the locked door.

Her heart pounding, she turned in that direction. The figure tried to sink further into the darkness. Dani knew who it was immediately when she saw the tell tale overnight bag hanging from his hand.

She stood there for a few minutes waiting for James to leave.

Once he left she went over to the door, trying the handle again. It started to turn, and then the lock clicked as if someone had turned it. A blast of cold air passed behind her. The candles flickered, then died.

Dani turned, placing her back against the door. She broke out in a cold sweat. Her eyes tried to adjust to the darkness, but they couldn't focus on anything. The only sound she heard was her own ragged breathing, coming in gasps as she tried to get her bearings.

That's when she felt it—the brush of a cold hand against her cheek. So light she though she was mistaken at first—that maybe it was just a piece of her hair.

When she felt it again, there was no mistaking it. Icy, gnarled fingers moved over her face, letting the nails scratch across her cheek.

Dani held her breath, her eyes tightly shut. The last thing she remembered before she screamed and slipped to the floor was a rasping voice in her ear. "Leave or end up like me".

A hand snaked out of the darkness to touch Dani's head. It rested there for a second then twined its fingers tightly around a few strands of hair. As the sound of footsteps approached, the hair was yanked from her head.

"Dani, Dani, can you hear me?"

She heard Parker's voice calling her name, but no sound escaped her lips.

Her eyes flickered open to find Parker and Hiram standing over her. The lamps were relit and she could see everything clearly. Finding herself lying on a bed, she searched her mind to remember what took place.

"What happened? Where am I?"

"You're in your room. We heard you scream and found you lying on the floor in the hall," Parker answered.

"Was anyone else there?"

"Just you on the floor unconscious. It scared the hell out of me! Are you okay?"

"Yes, I think so." She sat up and looked around.

"What happened to you Dani?" Hiram asked.

"Are you sure there wasn't anyone in the hall with me? All the candles blew out and it was dark. Maybe you just didn't see them."

The two men glanced at each other then back at her, confusion evident on their faces.

"Dani, it wasn't dark in the hall. All the candles were still lit when we found you."

"That isn't possible. The wind blew them out right after I saw James lurking in the shadows. Someone touched my face and whispered in my ear. They were trying to scare me." She tried desperately to make them believe her.

Parker tried to calm her down. "I believe you Dani. I just didn't see any of that. All I saw was you lying on the floor."

Dani scooted to the edge of the bed and stood. Her legs felt like jelly but she kept her footing.

"Something happened in that locked room. The door was open when I tried it and someone locked it so I couldn't get in. Then they tried to scare me away. I'm telling you something is going on here."

"Well I'd have to agree with that. I tried to tell you earlier when I showed you the pictures I've taken."

"What *is* that?" She looked at the camera Parker held in front of her.

"I can't say for sure, but it's only in the pictures I've taken of you since we got here. If you zoom in though it kind of looks like a face, not clear enough to really see anything in detail, but it has some hint of facial features."

Parker manipulated the camera and handed it to Dani.

She studied the picture and could see what he was talking about. In the center of the dark area near her head, she made out something that looked like a nose and further up a hair line. She wondered if they were reading more into it than they should.

The three of them stood in silence before finally agreeing to go downstairs for dinner. At the top of the second floor staircase, Hiram stopped

"I have to go get something," he said. "I'll meet you downstairs."

Dani and Parker continued down the stairs.

Hiram, however, didn't enter his room. Going back upstairs to the locked door, he couldn't resist the urge to turn the knob.

It wouldn't budge.

He examined the door in great detail, hoping to find a way to get into it. Pressing his ear against the hard wood he listened intently.

He heard nothing.

Dani said someone had touched her, but that could have been anyone. There were a number of people on the tour. She could have gotten spooked and allowed her imagination to run wild. He wanted to believe her, but as a scientist, he dealt in facts. Smacking his hand against the door he said, "Why is it happening to her and not me?"

Sitting in the dining area eating their dinner, Dani and Parker looked around at the people joining them.

"Still no sign of Kassandra—she must have turned in for the night," Dani said.

"That's probably a blessing, I don't think I could take any more of her constant chattering."

Hiram joined them and they ate their meal in silence until Jennifer Brooks walked up to them.

"Is everything going okay, the accommodations comfortable?" she asked.

"Yes," they said simultaneously.

"Are there any new developments on the transportation situation?" Parker put a hint of hope in his tone. He wanted out of this place and off this mountain as soon as humanly possible.

"No, I'm sorry. The storm still hasn't let up, and until it does, I'm afraid we are stuck here. Hopefully only a couple of nights, and I will try my best to make it a pleasant stay for all of you."

"We understand Miss Brooks. You have been very helpful. I appreciate you taking over earlier and informing Kassandra that we had to stay here," said Dani.

Jennifer's eyes scanned the room then settled back on Dani.

"I never could find Kassandra to tell her. Someone else must have informed her of our change of plans. Have any of you seen her?"

"No, not since I talked to you earlier. We assumed you had spoken to her and she had found a room."

"Someone must have informed her by now. It's nearly nine and we're all still here so she has to have asked someone what happened. This is a big place —it's easy to lose track of people." Jennifer fidgeted with her belt. She turned and walked away from the table.

By ten, very few guests remained in the dining room. Most had retired for the night.

"I guess we should head to bed too." Parker was still not thrilled with the idea of spending the night.

"I'm looking forward to sinking down into that big bed upstairs. It's been a long day," Dani answered.

They went upstairs, dropped Hiram off at his room then continued up to the third floor.

"I don't mind staying in your room Dani, if it would make you feel better. I could bunk down on the couch. I promise I'll be a gentleman." Parker grinned, trying to make light of the situation but he knew Dani was scared. Heck, he was scared himself. The blood-curdling scream she'd let out earlier nearly stopped his heart. Something had terrified her.

"I hate for you to have to sleep on the couch when you have that inviting bed waiting for you right next door," she said without much conviction.

"I insist. Just let me get my things and I'll be right back." He didn't give her a chance to refuse.

Parker grabbed his bag and was back in seconds.

Dani stared at the locked door, her eyes drifting to the bottom, looking for the light she had seen earlier. She shook her head and entered her room, Parker following close behind.

He watched in silence as she folded her arms around her trying to ward off the chill that seemed to be everywhere in the room. Settling himself on the couch, he watched Dani climb up into the big four poster and lay down staring at the ceiling. The lamps had nearly flickered out, their last bit of light dancing on the ceiling and walls.

"Thanks for staying with me."

"I'm not doing it for you—I'm doing it for me. I don't want to stay in that room by myself," he said.

She grinned in the dim light as her eyes closed and she drifted off to sleep.

* * * *

Dani's eyes flew open, but she didn't move. Darkness surrounded her. She tried to let her eyes adjust and could barely see shadows coming into focus.

It was cold, colder than it should have been and the memory of what happened earlier in the day came back to her.

That's when she saw the figure standing next to the bed.

Dani's heart pounded so hard she could hear it. She wanted to scream but her voice locked in her throat. Trying to lift her arms, she realized nothing would move no matter how hard she tried.

The dark figure inched closer to the bed, hovering closer and closer to her face.

It was too dark to make out any details, not that her brain could have registered anything, she was so terrified. She felt as though the life was being sucked right out of her.

As suddenly as it appeared, it was gone.

Dani sat straight up in bed, tears rolling down her face. Before she could even think to move, a loud bang echoed in the hall outside her room.

She jumped from the bed, bolted for the door, and ran straight into a hard muscled chest.

Kicking and punching Dani tried to get free from the arms that encircled her like a vice.

"Dani, it's me Parker!" he yelled.

She continued to struggle.

"Dani!"

She finally recognized Parker's voice. Relaxing in his arms she wept, tears streaming down her cheeks, wetting his shirt.

"It's okay, I'm here." He patted her back as she trembled in his embrace.

"Someone is in the room. They were standing right over me."

Heart pounding, Parker felt his way to the lamp and lit it.

As the room filled with light he glanced around cautiously. He didn't see anyone, but he checked every possible place a person could hide.

"There's no one here." Parker returned to her side. "The door is the only way out and I was standing right there. I would have seen if someone left the room. Maybe it was just a dream."

"No, it wasn't a dream. The same person was there in the hall when I fainted. They touched my face that time and talked to me."

"What did they say?"

"They told me to leave or end up like them."

"What in the hell does that mean?"

"I don't know, but I need to find out. I can't help but feel the answer is in that locked room and I intend to find a way in there."

* * * *

James sat alone in the library poring over the book in front of him.

There were spells in this book he had never seen. Concentrating intently, he didn't notice anyone in the room until arms wrapped around him and he felt his head sink into the cushioning warmth of his mate's breasts.

James leaned back and accepted the kiss she planted on his lips.

"Are you tired of hiding in the shadows, love?"

"Yes, I am darling." Kassandra sat herself in his lap.

"It won't be much longer. Then we can perform the ritual that will ensure your immortality. For now though, you must return to the room and stay out of sight. It was a risk for you to leave yesterday to scare that young lady. As long as they're looking for you, no one will have time to worry about anything else."

"I never left the room, James. You told me not to, so I stayed put."

"I thought you had done something to scare her. I guess she just got spooked and fainted." He stroked the book in front of him, then sent her on her way.

James read throughout the night, absorbing all he needed to complete his task. As the sun rose and the last of the warmth trickled from the fireplace, he closed the book. Standing, he lifted his bag to the desk and opened it a crack. He pulled the handkerchief from his pocket, checked to make sure the last thing required was still there, then folded it back up and placed it and the strands of jet black hair into the bag.

* * * *

The night was long for Dani and Parker. Neither of them slept much. They talked and speculated on how to get into the locked room, until exhausted, they both drifted off to sleep. It was a fitful sleep for Dani, interrupted by dreams that had no meaning to her. She got flashes of a young girl walking through the woods, then again strolling through the village.

Intermingled with that dream were visions of the same girl tied to a bed, covered in blood, screaming, while a shadowed figure danced around her.

Early in the morning they were awakened by claps of thunder and flashes of lightening streaking the sky. The rain had not let up during the night. Jennifer didn't have to tell any of them that the bus would not be returning today.

After breakfast, some of the guests gathered in the library to pass the time reading.

"Let's join the others in the library," Dani said.

"What for?" Parker asked.

"I don't know exactly, but there have to be clues to this castle and its previous occupants somewhere. The library is as good a place as any to look."

They ran across a journal written in the early 1600's listing the servants that were in residence at the castle, their dates of birth and their duties. Dani poured over the names until she came across a young lady named Luiza. From her birth date she would have been nineteen years old at the time the entry was made in the journal. The name seemed familiar to Dani. She didn't know anyone with that name, but maybe she had heard it on one of their outings in the village.

"There isn't anything here that's going to help me figure this out," Dani said. "Let's go check out some of the other rooms on this floor."

"Great, more creepy places to explore, I can't wait."

Together, they went through the hallways extending off the main hall. They discovered a wine cellar at the end of the first hall filled with bottles of old wine in one section and newer bottles in the other section. It was well stocked for guests and Parker had to contain himself from sneaking a bottle to drink later. Most of the halls led to rooms of little importance to Dani. There were no clues to the mysteries of the castle in any of them.

"There isn't anything down here, let's go to the second floor and see what we can find," Dani said.

"Lead on, I'm right behind you."

They hadn't seen Hiram all morning, so they were surprised to find him opening the door to his room when they reached the second floor.

"Where have you been hiding out?" Parker asked.

"I slept later than I planned but did have a chance to do some exploring this morning. What about you guys?"

"The same thing, we did a little exploring," Dani answered.

"Have either of you seen any sign of Kassandra?"

"No, we haven't, and I find that very disturbing even though she is a bit annoying," Parker answered. "How could she just disappear like that?"

"Surely Miss Brooks must have found her by now," Hiram said.

"Probably so." Dani nodded "I will ask her about it when I see her."

With that they parted, Hiram entering his room and Dani and Parker continuing with their explorations of the second floor.

* * * *

Hiram settled at the desk in his room and took out his calculator and a small notebook he carried in his pocket. His morning had been spent trying to find another way into the locked room. Examining its placement carefully and observing the structure of the building, it had come to him the room did not have a side connecting to an outer wall of the castle. It appeared to be self-contained within the castle itself. Hiram had calculated and figured there must be something between the room and the outer wall of the castle.

Going down to the kitchen he poked around and discovered a door inside the pantry that had been added since the kitchen was remodeled. He placed his hand on the knob, turned it, heard a click, then opened it.

He could see nothing in the darkness. He searched the kitchen, found a candle, lit it, and returned to the pantry.

Pushing the door wide so he could fit through, Hiram was delighted to find a staircase that wound up to the third floor—exactly where he thought it would.

After climbing, he found another door and tried the knob… locked. This particular piece of the puzzle now made him realize that someone would have ample time to climb these stairs, lock and unlock the hallway door, then retreat down the back stairs. This was turning out to be another fluke like all the others. Once, just once, he would love to find clear evidence that the paranormal does exist.

* * * *

Having exhausted all efforts to find anything on the second floor, Dani and Parker found themselves back on the third floor. When they reached the upper level, Dani felt chills run up and down her spine, her heart began to pound and she felt as though about to pass out. Parker held on to her arm and led her over to the seating area.

"What's wrong Dani?"

"I don't know. The closer I get to that room the more fearful I become. I get filled with dread at the thought of going in there, yet I feel like I have to also."

"The sooner we get out of here the better. Until then I'm not letting you out of my sight."

Jennifer came up the stairs as they spoke.

"There you are. I've been looking for you Miss Jamison. Where is the locked door you asked me about?"

"Come with me and I'll show you."

They walked down the hall, stopping before the door. Jennifer produced a ring with keys on it.

"We still haven't found Kassandra," Jennifer said, "and I thought…well, she might have inadvertently locked herself in here. These are the only keys I've found. I don't know which key belongs to what door, but I figured it was worth a try."

Hiram came up as they were trying to open the door. He wondered if any of the keys on the ring would open the door in the kitchen pantry. He didn't say anything because he didn't want anyone else knowing the door was there or the stairs. There was no way for him to control the factors he was speculating on if everyone had access to the back door of the room.

No one realized he was there so he turned and went back down the stairs.

They tried every key on the ring—none of them fit. They tried knocking and calling to Kassandra but got no response. Finally they gave up.

"I'm going to call Bruce," Jennifer said, "and let him know what's happened. There is no way for the authorities to get up the mountain any sooner than the bus driver can, but Bruce can let them know what's going on." She headed toward the stairs.

Parker was true to his word. He followed Dani around the rest of the day until she thought she'd scream. She appreciated him wanting to protect her, but she felt smothered.

It was nearly dark outside and Dani wasn't looking forward to another night of restless sleep, but she couldn't stand another second of Parker's hovering either. He and Hiram were playing a card game with a couple of the other guests, so Dani took that opportunity to slip away. She went to the kitchen, made herself a sandwich and carried it upstairs to eat in her room.

Standing in front of her bedroom door, she heard a scraping noise. Turning her head, she glanced at the locked door. In the dim light of the hallway she noticed the door was ajar. Thinking she'd imagined it at first, her mouth went dry when the scraping started again just as her eyes registered two legs sticking out of the open doorway.

The plate with the sandwich fell from her cold, numb fingers.

She turned toward the door in disbelief. With a final effort the stocking clad legs, kicking frantically, were pulled inside the room. The sound of the door slamming shut nearly deafened her.

Dani ran to the door, turning the knob frantically. It wouldn't budge.

"Help! Please, someone help me!" Dani yelled.

Hearing voices coming from inside the room, she pressed her ear against the door.

A woman screamed, but the sound of her voice became muffled.

Dani beat on the door with her fists trying to get it open so she could help the woman. Her efforts were useless.

"Kassandra? Kassandra is that you?"

James came up the steps at that moment and darted to the locked room. He watched as Dani frantically tried to get into the room, yelling for some invisible person to release the girl and leave her alone. Opening his bag, he took out a rag, poured a bit of chloroform on it and walked up behind her.

Dani turned.

"Thank God you're here. I just saw someone pulled into this room screaming. It may be Kassandra. We need to get some help."

James stared at her. She must have lost her mind. He was the only one with a key to the door. No one else could possibly be in there other than Kassandra. She was getting the room ready.

"Don't just stand there. Go get some help!" Dani yelled.

Before she knew what was happening, James grabbed her, holding the rag to her face. Her struggles were in vain.

An unconscious Dani in his arms, James opened the door and carried her in, still clutching his bag. He settled her on the bed; made sure everything in the room was ready, then opened the bag and removed his black-handled dagger, cloak, black candles and Dani's hair.

* * * *

The girl, Luiza, was hiding in the library when Lord Erdely found her. He dragged her kicking and screaming to the servants' quarters. Unlocking the door he pulled her by one arm into the room.

Stripping her clothes from her body he tied her to the bed, the ropes cutting into her flesh as she struggled to get free. Black candles flickered all around her, their shadows creating terrifying reflections on the ceiling and walls. Cloaked in black he stood before her, wand in hand. He held a chalice in the other hand and as he chanted the words needed to conjure his spell he poured blood over her body. Luiza screamed and screamed but there was no one to come to her aid.

* * * *

Dani felt the girl's terror and fought to wake from the terrifying dream that engulfed her.

Opening her eyes she realized she had awakened from one nightmare only to find herself in another. The bite of the ropes on her wrists and ankles made her scream as the cold air brushed over her naked flesh. Black candles flickered around her, their putrid smell burning her nose.

Painted above her on the ceiling was a large circle with a six pointed star in the center, words written around the outside of the circle.

Two cloaked figures stood next to the bed. Beyond terror, beyond being able to fight, she lay there quietly taking it all in, hoping to wake. One figure raised a black handled knife above her and she thought for a second it was going to plunge into her heart. A male voice called on Satan, the prince of darkness, to come into the room and grant him what he sought. In the other hand the man held a wand.

The other cloaked figure produced a golden chalice and held it over Dani.

Dipping the wand into the chalice, both figures began reciting as blood dripped from the wand onto Dani's flesh. As they invoked the spirits, they splashed blood from the chalice over her quivering body.

A fierce wind blew into the room, snuffing out all the candles except for the black ones.

A third cloaked figure appeared behind the other two. Dani wanted to close her eyes but she couldn't. This figure, much larger than the others, towered over them.

The two original figures turned once they realized someone was behind them. As soon as they did they were grabbed around their throats and lifted from the floor, their legs dangling wildly.

The cloaks fell from their heads and Dani watched in horror as James was tossed across the room. Kassandra's blonde hair whipped back and forth as that awesome figure choked the life from her body. Tossing her aside, the remaining figure stood over Dani, his arms outstretched, the cloak held out at his sides like wings. He covered her, his voice calling on Lucifer, his god. Her mind unable to handle any more, she slipped into oblivion.

* * * *

The ambulance pulled off from the castle grounds, its lights flashing but with no siren. The paramedics were in no rush to get James and Kassandra anywhere.

Dani sat in the library surrounded by Parker and Hiram. She hadn't said much since the incident.

They found it hard to believe she had gone through this ordeal and come out unharmed. There wasn't much she could tell the authorities. She simply didn't remember and everyone felt that was probably for the best. From what they could gather, James had kidnapped Dani with the intention of raping her. Kassandra, who they found out was married to James, caught him and they had fought. James had accidentally broken her neck and somehow fallen on his own knife, plunging it into his heart.

No mention was made of the ritualistic nature of the whole thing.

"Are you sure you're okay, Dani?"

"Yes, Parker, I'm fine. Stop hovering."

"Can I get you anything?"

"No, I'm fine, really." She was uncomfortable with all the attention.

Parker was glad Dani didn't remember anything and seemed unaffected by what had happened. Hiram had discovered where Dani was the night before and alerted everyone. He was the hero of the day but preferred to stay in the background and remain quiet. He had no intention of letting on that he saw the whole thing from the back stairwell.

Hiram was still in disbelief that he'd actually encountered a real spirit, something to work on to further his scientific research. He saw no point in sharing that with anyone just yet.

The bus arrived and the remaining guests were loaded on board.

Jennifer closed the large castle doors, followed the others and boarded the bus.

Everyone chatted as the bus pulled away, heading down the drive to take them back to the town of Cornifu. Everyone that is except Dani, who sat in silence, eyes unseeing, completely deaf to the conversations going on around her.

AUTHOR'S BIO: Donna Amato is a nurse who works with transplant patients. Her stories have been published in a variety of online and print magazines and two anthologies. She lives with three of her children in Shreveport, Louisiana and is currently working on her first novel. She can be reached at http://luvs2writela.tripod.com/

www.ingramcontent.com/pod-product-compliance
Lightning Source LLC
LaVergne TN
LVHW020648100826
845148LV00012B/2375